Dynamite versus Q.E.D.

Léo Malet was born in M
education and began as a
in Montmartre in 1925. H
to various magazines: *L'I*
Sandales . . . He had sever
manager of a fashion maga
seller . . .

From 1930 to 1940 he belonged to the Surrealist Group and was a close friend of André Breton, René Magritte, and Yves Tanguy. During that time he published several collections of poetry.

In 1943, inspired by the American writers Raymond Chandler and Dashiell Hammett, he created Nestor Burma, the Parisian private detective whose first mystery *120, rue de la Gare* was an instant success and marked the beginning of a new era in French detective fiction.

More than sixty novels were to follow over the next twenty years. Léo Malet won the 'Grand Prix de la Littérature policière' in 1947 and the 'Grand Prix de l'humour noir' in 1958 for his series 'Les nouveaux mystères de Paris', each of which is set in a different *arrondissement*. *Dynamite versus Q.E.D.*, the second Nestor Burma mystery, is set in 1942 and was first published in 1945.

Léo Malet lives in Châtillon, just south of Paris.

Léo Malet

Dynamite versus Q.E.D.

translated from the French by Peter Hudson
General editor: Barbara Bray

Pan Books
London, Sydney and Auckland

First published in France in 1945 as
Nestor Burma contre CQFD

Published in France in 1985 by Editions Fleuve Noir
This edition first published in Great Britain 1991 by
Pan Books Ltd, Cavaye Place, London SW10 9PG

9 8 7 6 5 4 3 2 1

ISBN 0 330 318489

Phototypeset by Intype, London

Printed in England by Clays Ltd, St Ives plc

to Louis Chavance
who set me on the path to crime

Contents

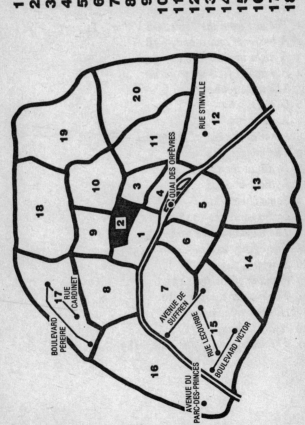

1 Louvre
2 Bourse
3 Temple
4 Hôtel-de-Ville
5 Panthéon
6 Luxembourg
7 Palais-Bourbon
8 Elysée
9 Opéra
10 Entrepôt
11 Popincourt
12 Reuilly
13 Gobelins
14 Observatoire
15 Grenelle/Vaugirard
16 Passy / Auteuil
17 Batignolles-Monceau
18 Butte-Montmartre

QUAI DES ORFÈVRES

RUE STINVILLE

RUE CARDINET

BOULEVARD PEREIRE

AVENUE DE SUFFREN

RUE LECOURBE

BOULEVARD VICTOR

AVENUE DU PARC-DES-PRINCES

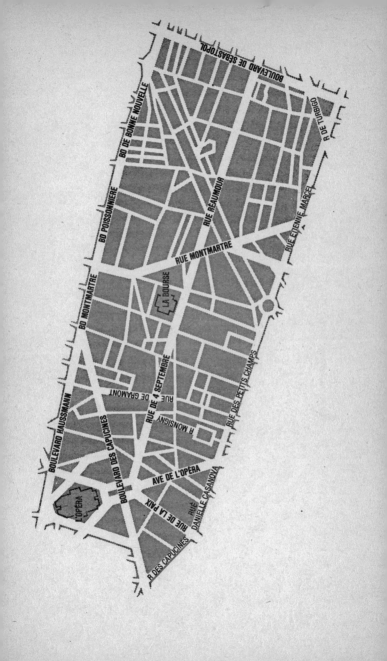

1 The girl from the boulevard Victor

Even if my pouch hadn't been empty that day, a man by the name of Briancourt would still have been plugged full of lead – two 7.65 mm bullets, to be precise. Only I wouldn't have been involved. But it so happened that on the morning of 17 March 1942 I'd been out of tobacco for twenty-four hours.

As a result I'd done nothing but loll at my desk in a state of catalepsy, wondering, not for the first time, how I'd ever acquired my nickname. 'Dynamite'.

I'd no idea how to help myself. Before I could hit on an idea of any kind I had to have a smoke. A vicious circle if ever there was one.

Luckily my secretary wasn't there just to show the Fiat Lux Agency's few clients what a good judge I was of female beauty. Hélène Chatelain's pretty little head was as resourceful as her heart was kind. So when she saw the state I was in she took matters into her own hands and phoned my journalist friend, Marc Covet. He told her there was a waiter called Jean at the Penguin Café on the boulevard du Lycée in Vanves who had connections. He specialized in shag.

I didn't need telling twice.

*

When I came out of the Penguin I had three packets. I emptied one straight into my pouch, filled my pipe and lit up. With the first puff I was a new man.

I looked on quite benignly now as a group of housewives queuing outside a shop bickered over which ration cards had priority. They suddenly seemed really charming. As I couldn't hear what they said I put their squawking down to sheer high spirits.

A bored-looking policeman standing on the kerb, either on duty or waiting for some housemaid to sneak a few minutes off, struck me as a very decent fellow. Maybe he wasn't even a genuine copper!

The sun had more strength to it now than when I'd left the office, and the studs on the pedestrian crossings shone like new pins. Spring was really on its way.

After a whole day spent sucking an empty pipe I had no intention of plunging back into the Métro, where smoking is so foolishly forbidden. Besides, I was in no hurry. I planned my route with the help of the map by the Underground station and started sauntering along with my hands in my pockets, well disposed towards the world in general.

When I got to the Porte de Versailles I checked my watch by the station clock. If the time was really five to eleven I was slightly fast – but at that point a dull drone seemed to arise from every point of the compass at once, and then, before I could identify it, swelled up into an appalling racket right overhead.

The dark shape of an aircraft, a black cross on the underside of each wing, swerved away over the Exhibition Centre at not much more than tree height and disappeared in the direction of the Auteuil viaduct.

This apparition set off a whole association of ideas: the war, the recent air raids and, the weather being so clear, the possibility of more. I'm afflicted with a sort of second sight, and don't remember ever having thought of the word 'alert' without the sirens going off immediately afterwards. My gift didn't fail me now.

No sooner had I crossed the road to look in the window of a bookshop I'd spotted near the corner of the boulevard Victor and the rue Desnouettes than the familiar wail started up.

I swore inwardly, and went on trying to decipher the price tag on a book that interested me. But I was wasting my ingenuity, for when I went to open the door I found the handle had been removed. A notice informed would-be customers that the shop opened only in the afternoons. So I went back to have another look in the window. And it was then that the young woman ran into me.

The bookshop formed part of a block of buildings facing on to the boulevard Victor, and I was so close to its main entrance that she could hardly avoid me as she burst forth into the street. She rushed past like a whirlwind on long, elegant legs encased in silk stockings you didn't often see the like of in wartime. Her high heels made no noise. She was wearing a blue suit and a golden astrakhan jacket that matched her auburn hair. I got only a glimpse of her face, but that didn't look ugly either. In short, she cut an intriguing figure as she swept away – and I'd rarely seen anyone in such a hurry.

Once I'd recovered from my surprise I got moving too. The sound of the sirens had been succeeded by a dull throbbing in the sky: the throaty roar of a squadron of bombers. Then a nearby anti-aircraft battery opened up, and, as if at a signal, others followed. The noise was deafening; like a myriad giant whip-cracks.

I'd closed in on the girl and was almost on her heels when shrapnel started raining down.

'What a bitch!' I exclaimed, so loudly it was audible even above the gunfire.

The girl spun round as though she'd been bitten by a snake.

I laughed.

'I didn't mean you!' I said. 'I was referring to the war in general, and to the law of gravity in particular. All this scrap metal we chuck up has to come down again somewhere.'

She shrugged and set off again.

She must have been about twenty, and she really was pretty, with a slender nose and well-formed mouth. But beneath her discreet make-up she looked pale, and from the way her large brown eyes had stared at me from between their magnificent lashes I could tell she was afraid. Perhaps because of the air raid. Anyway, being scared only made her more attractive.

We both quickened our pace, and I was still behind her when we got to the rue Lecourbe, where a policeman and an air-raid warden with a tin helmet several sizes too big for him popped up like a couple of jack-in-the-boxes. The policeman was blowing a whistle, but took it out of his mouth to shout at us.

'Cover! Take cover! Are you deaf? . . . Don't you know there's a raid on?'

'All right,' I said. 'Don't get worked up. We were just looking for a shelter. Where's the nearest?'

'Over there!' he bawled, pointing at a building a few yards away.

I set off obediently.

'You too, madame,' said the warden in a voice more polite than the policeman's but just as firm. I turned round to see that the girl hadn't followed my example. On the contrary, she was showing every sign of continuing on her way. Unfortunately for her they were sticklers for the rules in this neighbourhood, perhaps because there were some government offices nearby. At any rate, the two men planted themselves in front of her and barred her path.

'Please!' she said. 'I've got a train to catch!'

She had a pleasant, musical voice, now tinged with anxiety.

'That's nothing to do with me,' said the policeman. The other nodded in agreement. His tin hat almost fell off.

'Into the shelter with you,' he said.

The girl tried to force her way past.

'The shelter, we said.' It was the policeman's turn now.

'But please, officer,' she implored.

'*Will* you get into the shelter!'

Just at that moment a large piece of shrapnel landed less than a yard away. The cop laid a brawny hand on the girl's fur coat.

'If you don't do as you're told I'll slap a fine on you and take you down to the station into the bargain,' he growled.

From the entrance to the house now designated as a shelter, a small crowd was watching these goings on with great amusement.

'He'd do it, too, the devil,' one of them said. 'It wouldn't be the first time.'

The girl seemed to resign herself to the inevitable, and we moved towards the door. I smiled at her as I stepped back to let her go in first, but she remained stony-faced.

'Bit of an ogre, isn't he?' I said.

She didn't even turn her head, just shrugged contemptuously as she had before in the street. Our conversations seemed doomed to be brief and to the point.

The anti-aircraft fire had now redoubled in violence. Shell fragments were hurtling down like hail outside, and an explosion nearby rattled the windows of the concierge's *loge*. The policeman and the warden joined us in the entrance. The cop still hadn't got over the way the girl had stood up to him.

'So,' he said to her sarcastically. 'You think it's the right sort of weather for a stroll, do you?'

Then he noticed the rest of us for the first time.

'What are you all hanging around up here for?' he said. 'Tired of living, or what? Get down into the shelter, for God's sake. Go on!'

Another explosion lent force to his argument. A door slammed as though caught in a gust of wind, and somewhere higher up the stairwell a window blew in with a crash. Fragments of blue glass landed at our feet.

'It *would* be wiser,' I said. The first time in my life I'd ever agreed with a cop.

The basement was large and well lit, with a central passageway and individual cellars leading off it on either side. Two women, who'd obviously been there since the warning sounded, were sitting on soap boxes. The elder of the two was muttering to herself; the other was clutching a baby. She looked terrified, but the infant, bundled up tightly, was fast asleep with its thumb in its mouth.

We settled down among the rest as best we could. There weren't more than ten of us, including the old girl who'd shouted out to us about the policeman. She seemed to have a grudge against him, and reeled off a string of anecdotes about what a terror he was: very hot on cyclists, rear lights, and such like, but with a soft spot for air raids because they made him feel important. We'd seen as much ourselves, hadn't we? One day he'd come down and searched everyone in the shelter, men and women alike, and all because someone had answered him back. If she'd been in the government . . .

At least she gave everyone a good laugh. Or almost.

Although the sound was muffled by the time it reached us, the din up above continued unabated, and some of the faces around me were deadly serious. The old woman was still muttering, the younger one looked as solemn as ever, and the girl who'd been in such a hurry wasn't any better. She paced up and down the passage, nervously turning back her glove to look at her watch. As for one man leaning against the wall at the bottom of the stairs, you only had to look at him to see he wished it was all happening to somebody else.

Suddenly we were rocked by a bigger explosion than any that had gone before, and the lights went out.

There was a volley of oaths and a woman shrieked.

'We're for it this time,' someone remarked flatly.

'It's the ministry they're after,' said someone else, trying to sound cheerful.

Then there was a click and the lights came on again.

'Don't worry – it was only me,' stammered the fellow at the foot of the stairs, obviously rather ashamed of himself. 'I was leaning against the wall . . . and I slipped and turned the switch off by mistake.'

We all breathed a sigh of relief. The damage couldn't be so bad if the power was still on.

The smell of Virginia tobacco made me turn round. The 'girl in a hurry' was calmly drawing on a *Fashion* cigarette. To judge by how little of it she'd smoked she must have lit it only a moment ago, while the lights were out. And yet I didn't remember seeing the flame from a match or a lighter.

2 A bedroom and a body

A few minutes went by. They seemed like centuries. The old girl's tittle-tattle was forgotten and everyone had fallen silent except the baby, who'd been woken by the explosion, and its mother, who was trying to console it. The baying of the anti-aircraft batteries was now almost inaudible. The nearest ones had shut down altogether. With the danger apparently past and everything quiet again, I left the shelter and went upstairs. As I reached the entrance hall I heard a familiar double note, and a red fire engine went hurtling past down the street.

When I ventured out on to the pavement it was as empty as on a bank holiday. The only person in sight was the policeman, standing with his back to the wall waiting for the peace treaty to be signed. Then the long wail of the sirens broke the oppressive silence with the 'All Clear'.

'That last one sounded pretty close, didn't it?' I said.

The policeman took off his tin helmet, hooked it on to his belt, and called out to the warden, who was just coming round the corner.

'Two bombs in the rue Desnouettes,' the warden reported.

'The rue Desnouettes?'

It was the voice of the girl in a hurry, leading the rest of the group out of the shelter.

'Any damage?' someone else asked.

'Oh no,' said the warden sarcastically. 'They were only made of cardboard. One of them fell on a kitchen and blocked up the sink.'

'I'm serious!'

'So am I, for God's sake! Don't ask such stupid questions! Two houses were hit.'

'Whereabouts?'

'Near the boulevard.'

The girl's eyes widened.

'Good God,' said a passer-by. 'It wasn't number 103, was it? That's where I live.'

'No, I don't think it was 103,' said the warden vaguely.

The man decided he'd better go and see for himself, and set off at the double. The rest of the group broke up.

Meanwhile the girl in a hurry had crossed the street and was striding away as fast as ever towards the centre of town. The March sun struck copper lights from her hair. She'd awakened my interest in more ways than one. I had nothing particular to do.

So I followed her.

We went up the rue Lecourbe, then a little way along the avenue Suffren. She didn't look back once. Not worried about being tailed.

The Métro station at Sèvres-Lecourbe had only just been reopened after the air raid. It was twelve thirty-five p.m. The girl joined the crowd on the stairs leading down to the trains, and I was right behind her. I didn't want to get left behind if the gate to the platform suddenly closed.

It wasn't easy struggling down to the Nation line through all those people, but it could have been worse.

A train came in straight away and we got into the front coach. A spotty schoolboy, dazzled by such an apparition, blinked furiously at the girl, wondering how to impress her. He decided to be a gentleman and offer her his seat. The smile she gave him must haunt his dreams to this day.

I was still standing, and she sat down facing me. From time to time our eyes met, but her beautiful brown orbs showed as much interest in me as if I'd been a block of wood.

She must have been brought up at a convent school, though, because when a man with crutches got on at Pasteur she stood up and gave him the seat she owed to the smitten schoolboy.

There was a bit of pushing and shoving just before we got to Montparnasse, and I ended up trapped in the crowd further down the coach. The girl stayed put and I began to manoeuvre to get near her again. Then we came into the station.

A good few people got off, and a good few more got on. She was still there, and now we were separated only by a workman in overalls reading a newspaper. The doors began to close . . .

And then came a blast on a whistle.

I swore out loud.

At the very last moment she'd caught hold of the handles of the doors as they came together, and forced them apart just enough to allow her to jump out on to the platform. The train was already pulling away, and do what I might it was impossible for me to follow. The doors slammed in my face, and we were already in the tunnel.

I'd been had. Candy from a baby.

The stations at Edgar Quinet and Raspail were closed, so I got off at Denfert, changed to the Etoile line and finally emerged again at the Porte de Versailles. The girl's pluck and shrewdness in shaking me off had whetted my interest in what I sensed was the beginning of an adventure. For want of anything better to do I decided to have a look at the house she'd come out of when she bumped into me.

The bookshop was still closed. Although some bombs had fallen quite near by, it hadn't suffered any damage. I went down the passage the girl had come out of and found myself in a courtyard. I stopped and looked around to get my bearings. I wasn't sure which part of the building to start with.

Suddenly I thought I heard someone above me let out an exclamation of surprise. I looked up at the windows, but all I could see was a lot of rather grubby washing optimistically hung out to dry. Yet I was sure I hadn't been imagining things. To set my mind at rest I went in under a sort of archway and made for the stairs.

But a figure loomed out of the shadows. A policeman. I couldn't move today without falling over the law.

'Where do you think you're going?' he asked. 'Do you live here?'

I was just about to answer when someone else came hurrying down the stairs and a voice from above said:

'Hallo, Burma!'

The light from a window on the landing revealed a tall, gaunt figure with the face of a wily countryman and a prematurely grey moustache. He was wearing a light-coloured raincoat and a hideous brown felt hat. Inspector Florimond Faroux of the CID.

The policeman at the foot of the stairs had set my antennae going, but when I saw Faroux my heart really began to race. My intuition hadn't deserted me – sniffing around here had been a very good idea!

'Well, well,' I said. 'What are you in such a rush about? Running away from someone?'

'I spotted you from the window,' he said as we shook hands. 'You seemed to be looking for something. I was coming to see if I could be of any assistance.'

'That's very kind of you,' I said. 'Since when have you been playing the Good Samaritan?'

He didn't deign to reply.

'What are you doing here?' he asked.

'Nothing in particular. What about you?'

'The same.'

I began to laugh.

'When clam meets clam . . . !'

He repeated his question.

'Look here,' I said by way of reply, 'there must be something behind all this. You're not here collecting for the Red Cross. And this assistant of yours isn't on guard for nothing.'

'If you'd care to follow me,' Faroux said stiffly, 'I'll show you the explanation.'

He led me up to a furnished room at the top of the dark stairway. Three men, one of them in uniform, were busy with a fourth, who was lying stretched out on the carpet. He couldn't have been much disturbed by the sound of the explosions.

Two bullets had made their way into his stomach to see what he was made of, and decided not to come out again.

It was a depressing, featureless place, as chillingly impersonal as all furnished rooms the world over, while still bearing phantom traces of other lives. The walnut bed in the corner, the chest of drawers, the round table with its fringed cloth – they must all have represented the height of elegance at the time of the landlady's marriage, itself recorded in a yellowing plush-framed photograph that stood on the marble mantelpiece. According to the clock beside it, the time was twenty minutes past one.

A pair of underpants, a waistcoat and a grey tweed jacket, its right pocket turned inside out, hung over the back of a chair with a worn velvet seat. Two brown shoes with socks stuffed inside stuck out from under the unmade bed, over which an overcoat had been spread to make an extra blanket.

The dying embers of a small stove were fighting a losing battle against the cold air streaming through the window. The panes had been blown in during the air raid, and the man lying on the floor had been cut in the face by a splinter of flying glass.

Despite the sharpness of its features, accentuated now in death, it wasn't a disagreeable face. When it had been lit up by the green eyes now staring obliviously at a patch of damp on the ceiling, it must have made many a female heart beat faster. We were looking at a suburban Don Juan of about forty, whose hair was starting to go grey at the temples.

The corpse was dressed only in a shirt and trousers, its feet thrust into a pair of unfastened espadrilles.

As I took all this in, Florimond Faroux introduced me to the others present.

'This is Monsieur Nestor Burma,' he said.

All three faces turned towards me with interest. Flattering enough, but the atmosphere was uncomfortably tense. I couldn't make out why I was being given such an eager reception. No doubt time would tell.

I pointed the stem of my pipe at the corpse.

'What a pretty picture,' I said with more gusto than I felt. 'Who is it?'

'The name's Briancourt,' said Faroux.

'Henri Briancourt,' he added, as though this detail would open up untold horizons. 'An actor.'

'Oh,' said I. 'And who cast him in the role of victim? Whoever it is, I suppose you're counting on me to catch him.'

'Who said so?' said a dumpy fellow with a face so red it broke the blackout regulations. It was the local police chief. I turned to him with a smile.

'Nobody said so. But why else would an ordinary private detective like me be invited to come and inspect the scene of the crime? There must be a reason.'

'My dear Monsieur Burma,' he began. His sudden politeness was not convincing. 'Even if the official police and private operators are, as you insinuate, in perpetual conflict, we do share certain principles. One is that we leave no stone unturned.'

'I should say not!' I agreed.

'So when Inspector Faroux saw you out there in the courtyard he thought your evidence might be useful to us. You've rubbed shoulders with all sorts of people in the course of your career, and it's just possible—'

'That I might know this bloke?' I said.

'Exactly.'

'H'm . . . Some method!' I said. 'If you pick up all your witnesses on the off chance, I suppose you're bound to find the killer in the end. But there are forty million people in France. It could take some time.'

'Especially if they all like the sound of their own voice as much as you do,' said Faroux. 'Do you know this fellow or not?'

I said I realized he'd have liked me to say yes, but I couldn't trifle with the truth just to make him happy. He said he quite understood. Everyone knew Nestor Burma could never tell a lie.

At that moment two constables came in, one to report on his inquiries in the building, the other to announce the arrival of the police doctor and photographers. The new arrivals immediately took over, so I sat down in a corner, lit my pipe and kept my eyes and ears open. Apart from Faroux, who looked the occasional dagger, everyone seemed to have forgotten about me.

'You took your time,' said the local chief to the senior photographer.

'If you could see the car we've got you'd be congratulating us on how fast we were,' said the other.

'Anyway,' said Faroux, 'it doesn't make any difference. Your pictures won't show anything. About a dozen people found the body, and they trampled all over the place.'

The whole pack of them now started exchanging information, and I began to get some idea of what had happened.

A demolition squad at work in what remained of a nearby house had spotted the body through the shattered window and assumed the man was the victim of either a stray anti-aircraft shell or a bomb. So they'd hurried over, only to find that he'd been shot. Unfortunately, by this time they'd moved the body, and all their comings and goings had obliterated any traces that might have been left by the killer. So by the time Florimond Faroux, who just happened to be visiting the local police station, arrived on the scene with the superintendent, there was little hope of finding any clues.

Henri Briancourt's papers showed him to be aged forty-three and an actor, though he had no union card.

The room was sub-let to the actor by the tenant of the flat as a whole, a widow named Madame Planchon who was away. But according to the neighbours Briancourt had only been living there since the thirteenth, and had come, as far as they knew, from the unoccupied zone. He'd been a quiet man, both to talk to and in his habits, leaving the building regularly at midday and not returning home until just before the curfew. The only time he'd made any noise had been the previous day, coming up the stairs. He must have had one too many.

'Did you say he was an actor?' said one of the photographers as he snapped away. It transpired he was a bit of an expert on show business – not the sort to mix Harpo Marx up with Fernandel. But he said he'd never set eyes on this fellow, never even heard of him. Someone else suggested he might have done only character parts and acted under a pseudonym. But Faroux pointed out how limited his wardrobe was. He obviously didn't believe what the dead man's papers said, chiefly because of his bright yellow shoes, which Faroux clearly regarded as typical of a racketeer from the south.

The medics, after lengthy discussion, finally agreed that the shots that caused Briancourt's death had been fired in an upward direction at a distance of about eighteen inches from the body. The murderer must have been much shorter than the victim. The weapon was a Browning 7.65. This last detail was gleaned from the only shell-case they found that hadn't been flattened by the demolition workers' hobnailed boots. None of the neighbours had heard the shots.

Death had occurred recently, though the experts couldn't be precise about the time. Faroux and the local superintendent thought the noise of the detonations had probably been covered by that of the bombs. Briancourt had no doubt been getting up at his usual time when he was surprised by the murderer – a cool customer who'd deliberately planned to take advantage of the air raid.

I picked up a couple more pieces of information as they talked. Robbery wasn't the motive: ten thousand francs had been found on the table, and a little over two thousand in Briancourt's pocket. And there were two ways out of the building: one on to the boulevard Victor and the other via number 103, rue Desnouettes.

With that, the gods decided I knew enough. I saw Faroux and the superintendent whispering and glancing in my direction. Then the Inspector came over.

I took the bull by the horns.

'It's all very well to suspect me,' I said suavely, 'but—'

Faroux led me out on to the landing.

'I don't think you did it,' he said.

'What *did* I do, then?'

'I asked you a question,' he growled, 'the only one we wanted to ask you, and you wouldn't give a straight answer. It's up to you to reconsider your position. As far as I'm concerned, I've got nothing more to say.'

'Come, come, my friend,' I said, 'don't beat about the bush. Just tell me why you let me see the body. Why do you all think I knew Briancourt?'

'He's an ex-POW,' said Faroux slowly. 'He was repatriated because of his health, and demobbed at Marseilles on the tenth of this month. Here's his demob card,' he added, extracting it carefully from an envelope.

As I examined it, he went on:

'When I saw you in the courtyard, I thought he must be a mate of yours. I thought you'd come to see him – that perhaps you were in the same camp.'

'He was in Stalag VIII C,' I said, giving him back the card. 'I was in X B. They're more than a thousand miles apart.'

He put the envelope back in his pocket.

'Anything else?' I said.

He shrugged impatiently.

'We have no power to hold you. And even if we kept you in jug all night we wouldn't get anything out of you except some more of your so-called jokes. But we always know where to find you.'

'That's right,' I said. 'Come up and see me some time. And don't forget to keep asking me if I know Briancourt, or anyone else who gets himself bumped off in the course of the week.'

I was just about to turn away, but he grabbed me, his moustache bristling.

'If you didn't know Briancourt, what were you doing skulking about here?'

'Oh!' I said. 'So now we're getting down to brass tacks. Skulking, was I? Listen, Faroux, maybe you're just hungry. It's nearly three o'clock, and my stomach thinks my throat's cut, too. So, as you don't intend to keep me any longer, I'm going to get something to eat. But first I'll set your mind at rest about why I was in the courtyard. Come with me!'

A few moments later we were in the bookshop, now open at last, and I was buying a book that had attracted my attention earlier: Henri Pastoureau's *Cry of the Medusa*.

'It's very rare,' said the bookseller, and to prove it promptly added ten francs to the price pencilled inside (already double the original price).

'I know,' I said. 'That's why I've been waiting for you to open. You weren't there at a quarter past one.'

'No, monsieur,' he said. 'I've just opened this minute.'

'That's what I was doing in the courtyard,' I said to Faroux as we went out. 'I'd gone round the back to look for the bookseller. Cheerio.'

I just left him standing there, taking off so suddenly that I walked right into a member of the demolition squad who was having a breather and smoking a very pungent cigarette. On my way to the Métro I bought a newspaper which I knew had a reasonably easy crossword, and was trying to think of an eight-letter word meaning 'Not tame' when the train pulled out.

But I wasn't really in the mood. I filled in the clues mechanically, thinking of other things, and the eight-letter word took care of itself without any effort on my part. It was the adjective *farouche*, which can mean wild, savage or fierce. Another coincidence. Inspector Faroux had been rather savage with me. I started to doodle 'Farouche Inspector Faroux' in the margin of the paper. And then was lost in thought.

3 A night in Bois-le-Roi

Hélène greeted my return with a sigh of relief.

'Half-past three,' she said. 'I was getting worried. Tobacco will be your undoing. I hope you got what you were after.'

I said I had, went through into my office, and asked her to go and get me a sandwich from the café downstairs. As I waited for her to come back I stood by the window looking absent-mindedly down the boulevard, which was still bathed in sunlight. When she returned I sat and ate my sandwich, catching up on the mail that had come in while I was out: three letters and a rolled-up newspaper.

The first two envelopes contained advertisements and were of no interest. The third held out a welcome possibility of making some money. A would-be client who had doubts about his wife's fidelity wanted me to send him a man – not for his wife; she was already provided for – but for himself, to set on the faithless one's tracks. Hélène had pencilled 'Reboul' on the corner of the letter, and I approved her suggestion. Reboul was just the man for the job.

Then I lit my pipe and relaxed with the newspaper. It was *The Wire*, 'the mouthpiece of repatriated prisoners'. I'd taken out a subscription when I got back from POW camp.

On page 4, under the heading 'Missing', I read the following announcement:

No news of my son, Jean Alphonse Gremet, for several months. Registration number: 70123. Stalag XB. All information to his widowed mother, Madame Gremet, 32, rue Jean-Jaurès, Bois-le-Roi, Seine-et-Marne.

I opened a drawer and took out a piece of paper of the kind familiar to anyone with a relative or friend in a POW camp. It had come a week before from someone I'd got to know when I was a prisoner in Sandbostel, and whom I'd left behind there. His name was Jean Gremet. He was worried because he hadn't heard from his mother, and he wrote asking me to go and see her and let him know as soon as possible whether anything was wrong. He went into minute detail about how fed up he was, but omitted to give me his mother's address.

Luckily there were irregularities in the post in both directions, so as the old lady hadn't been getting *his* letters either, she'd decided to make use of *The Wire*. I made a mental note to go and see her one day soon and set both their minds at rest. Then the telephone rang.

I'd left the connecting door open, and could hear Hélène pick up the phone and say 'Hallo', and then 'Oh! Hallo, Monsieur Faroux'.

I scribbled 'I'm not here' on a scrap of paper, took it in, and thrust it under her nose.

'Er – Monsieur Burma's out,' she said. 'Yes, yes. He did come in at about half-past three, but he went straight out again. He didn't say when he'd be back . . . Yes, I'm afraid you'll have to call back later.'

She hung up.

'He seemed very anxious to see you,' she said, a gleam of curiosity in her grey eyes. 'What does he want?'

'Didn't he say?'

'No.'

'I don't know, then. Did he believe you?'

'I don't think so. He's known you for too long.'

I went over to the window, and Hélène came and stood beside me.

'Lovely day,' she said.

'Yes,' I said. 'Some people seem to be enjoying it. The chap you can see standing in front of the newspaper stand, for example. He was there just now when you went to get my sandwich.'

'I expect he doesn't like the cold. He's stocking up on sunshine.'

'And perhaps there's something else he'd like to stock up on.'

'Such as what?'

'I don't know,' I said. 'And I've no intention of asking.'

I went and put on my raincoat and hat.

'Faroux's going to turn up at any minute,' I said. 'I'm not at all keen to meet him. I'm going for a walk.'

The man outside started tailing me, so I had to lose him. That done, I took the Métro and reached the Gare de Lyon three minutes before the next train left for Fontainebleau.

I settled down in a corner of the compartment and soon became engrossed in the crossword I'd kept in my pocket to relieve my mind of more serious problems. I soon finished it, but this rare feat didn't go long unpunished. The train seemed to have left the sun behind over Paris, and the sky was growing overcast. At Alfortville I saw a woman open an umbrella as she crossed the bridge. The train went slowly, as though afraid of slipping on the damp rails. At this rate, I thought, we shan't be in Bois-le-Roi before nightfall. And that's how it turned out.

There was a long halt at Melun. Some problem on the track a couple of miles ahead. Every passenger had his own theory about what must have happened. I couldn't make out whether the trouble was due to a derailment, to the blowing up of a munitions train, to a shell-hole on the line, or to a plane having been shot down. Or to all four at once. I decided to do without the details, and went off to the station buffet.

Finally, amid much grumbling from the passengers, the train got going again.

I was the only passenger who alighted at Bois-le-Roi, a few minutes before blackout time according to my newspaper. A fine drizzle was falling, accompanied by gusts of wind, and the only signs of activity in the little station were due to the rattling of the roof and the fitful gleam of a single dimmed light.

There was a bar in the station square, so I went in to have a drink and ask my way. Having got this far I might as well carry the thing through. I only hoped Madame Gremet didn't go to bed too early.

According to the barman the rue Jean-Jaurès was quite a long way off, and difficult to find in the dark, especially if you didn't know the village. Unless . . .

'Hey, Arthur!'

Arthur was smoking his pipe at the other end of the bar. He looked like a local. Wasn't he going in that direction? He could take me part of the way. Just give him time to finish his ersatz Dubonnet and he'd be at my service.

There was no question of going back to Paris that night, so as this was a hotel as well as a bar I booked a room. I'd almost finished filling in the form when Arthur told me he was ready. I bought a round of drinks and we left.

Outside, Arthur walked straight into a privet growing in a tub. This sparked off a string of imprecations against the

33

weather, the war, and mankind in general, which continued all the time he was with me. By now it was quite dark. It was still raining, and there wasn't a star in the sky. You could hear the trees rustling in the wind.

After we'd been walking for a quarter of an hour my companion stopped dead. We'd long since left the streets behind and were walking along muddy lanes.

'This is where I live,' he said. 'But you can't go wrong from here. First on the left, then third on the right. Don't expect to find a street sign, though. Some right-wing yobs pulled it down last week and it hasn't been replaced yet. But you can't miss the place.'

So I went on alone.

I turned left as instructed and then started counting the streets, passing small detached houses that looked dreary and deserted because of the strict blackout. They were all guarded by ferocious dogs that strained at their chains and barked threateningly as I passed.

The further I went the denser the darkness seemed. Through the icy wind I could just hear the stirring of a nearby forest. A distant clock struck nine.

Gremet and his mother would never know what I'd suffered on their behalf . . . Though I had to admit it was Faroux who'd driven me out of my office.

In due course I turned into a street from which the sign had been removed – it had obviously borne the name of Jaurès, the famous socialist orator – and began, with the aid of my torch, to look for number 32. I found it at the corner of a little path that seemed to lead straight off into the country. It was a single-storey building raised above ground level, with five or six steps going up to the front door. On one of the gateposts I made out the number, almost illegible. The gate into the little front garden wasn't locked, so I went through without bothering to look for the bell.

On the last step but one of the flight leading up to the front door my rubber soles slipped and I lurched forward, throwing my arms out in front of me to cushion my fall. Beneath my weight the heavy front door swung gently open on to a dark passage. There was a faint smell of perfume. A door to the right was ajar, and from it came a narrow ray of light. I could hear a confused murmur of voices, mingled with groans. I approached silently and peered through the crack. What I saw brought a whistle of surprise to my lips. But I stifled it, made sure the front door was shut, grabbed my pistol, kicked open the inner door and burst into the room.

'Don't bother to get up,' I said. 'It's only me.'

Two men leapt to their feet and spun round to face me. One, who'd been twisting the wrist of a slim figure lying bound up on the sofa, let it drop from his hairy hand. He had the flattened features and flabby body of an over-the-hill boxer. Two eyes devoid of intelligence blinked at me from under the peak of his cloth cap.

His companion sported a thin moustache beneath his crooked nose. His hat was tipped back, revealing a receding forehead. His cruel, almost lipless mouth and chin receded too, and his cunning eyes were evasive. Mentally I nick-named him 'The Sloper'. His body was thin and agile; his suit well cut but showy. He was like a snake with a fox's head.

As for the person, bound at ankles and thighs, to whom they were devoting so much attention, it was none other than the girl from the boulevard Victor.

With another kick I closed the door behind me.

'Reach,' I said.

They put their hands up.

'What *is* this?' I said. 'A serenade or a ju-jitsu lesson?'

There was a glimmer of fear in the boxer's bleary eyes.

'Serenade?' he growled. 'Is this bloke barmy?'

'Shut up,' ordered 'The Sloper'. 'Let him jabber. That's all he's good for.'

'You've got it all wrong,' I said. 'You're the ones who are going to jabber. But first let's have your guns.'

Then I thought for a moment, without taking my eyes off them. It would be foolish to search them. While I dealt with one I'd be an easy target for the other. One of them was an ex-boxer who couldn't have entirely forgotten how to use his fists, and the other was a dirty little reptile, a-slither with tricks from his slicked-down hair to his patent-leather toes. He must already be working out the price he'd make me pay for interrupting their little game.

It was two against one.

Or was it?

The girl had sat up, and was trying to untie the ropes round her arms and legs. Wouldn't she be my ally? I'd got her out of a tricky situation, and though we hadn't hit it off too well up to now, surely we could come to some kind of limited agreement?

'Turn round,' I said to the two crooks, 'and face the lady.'

'Better than looking at you,' said 'The Sloper', obeying. 'Cut out the witty remarks.'

Still keeping them covered I went over to the sofa, and, half kneeling on it, spoke to the girl, not taking my eyes off the boxer and his mate. She knew very well what I wanted, and our non-aggression pact was concluded in a few seconds. However, my heart beat faster as I handed her the revolver. What was she going to do?

It wasn't the first time she'd held a gun. She levelled the Browning at the two men in a very business-like manner.

'Go ahead,' she told me.

I went behind 'The Sloper' and lifted his coat to get at his revolver pocket. With cat-like swiftness he drove his right arm back, catching me on the cheek with his elbow. I'd only eaten a sandwich that day and drunk a fair amount, so I didn't react too well. But I was soon straightened up by a tremendous blow to the chin from the boxer, who'd recovered his long-lost youth and thought he was back in the ring again. He gave me another hook to the stomach which made me forget my hunger cramps immediately, and down I went.

As I fell I clung to the Sloper's legs like a drowning man to a lifebelt. But the boxer, spitting oaths, dislodged me with a kick and I hit the floor for a couple of seconds. Just long enough for them to get away.

I scrambled up, hurled myself through the door and crashed down the steps into the night. A car with no lights on hurtled along the lane, almost knocking me down, and roared away into the rain-drenched darkness.

I was left with the smell of petrol in my nostrils, mud from the car all over my clothes, and fury in my heart. I yelled out an insult that echoed emptily into the distance.

A chink of light went out between two curtains in the house opposite. Someone who didn't want any trouble. I went back into number 32.

The girl was still trying unsuccessfully to untie herself. She'd put my revolver down beside her and I retrieved it without any trouble. Had she noticed it wasn't loaded? I'd bluffed the two men with it, but bluff can't work for ever. That's why I'd been in such a hurry to get hold of the loaded guns they were certainly carrying, and taken the risk of handing my own weapon over to the girl. But I'd been afraid the Sloper would smell a rat as soon as he saw me do it, and I must have been right. That's why he hadn't hesitated to go for me.

The girl stopped struggling with her bonds. Brown eyes gazed at me from beneath heavy lashes.

'Have they gone?' she said.

Her voice was throaty and exciting.

'Of course not,' I joked. 'They're still standing petrified with you pointing the Browning at them.' I took off my trench coat. 'Why didn't you shoot?' I asked with a tinge of reproach.

She didn't answer. Only looked down and began working at the ropes again. If she'd tried the trigger and realized the truth she wouldn't be behaving like this. As it was, she looked like a little girl caught with her hand in the biscuit tin.

'Why didn't you shoot?' I repeated, sitting down beside her.

'I . . . I don't know.'

'I told you to fire if they moved a finger, and they moved several.'

I rubbed my chin and stomach ruefully.

'You only had to move one. So why didn't you?'

'I don't know. Oh, damn!' She'd broken a nail trying to undo a knot.

'Let me help,' I said.

I took out my knife and cut through the ropes.

'Did you want to save one of them, or what?'

She swung her legs over, stood up, and began tottering about to get her circulation going again. Then she turned to me, her hair dishevelled and a look of anger in her eyes.

'What do you mean, "save one of them"? I'd never set eyes on them before. And they beat me up.'

'Precisely,' I said. 'What did they want?'

'I don't know.'

'You don't know much, do you?'

'No. I don't even know what you're doing here.'

'Me?' I said. 'I came to save you. I'm the guardian angel of pretty young ladies, the Don Quixote of 1942. Only a wartime substitute, but I serve the purpose. So when my intuition told me you were in danger, I came to get you out of it.'

'Of course,' she murmured. 'I believe every word you say. You've got such an honest face.'

I laughed as heartily as my painful jaw would permit.

'That's what all my friends say. You're pretty forthcoming yourself.'

She didn't reply; just examined the damage the ropes had done to her stockings. Then she stood up.

'I must look a mess,' she said. 'I'm going to change and freshen up a bit. With your permission, that is. You seem to be more at home here than I am.'

She appeared to be making the best of a bad job and accepting my presence without undue fuss. I congratulated myself inwardly and remarked that I thought this was Madame Gremet's house. Again she didn't answer.

I followed her into the next room, where she took a light-coloured dress out of the wardrobe and shut herself up in the bathroom. I sat on the bed to wait for her and looked about me.

The telephone stood on a low revolving bookcase that held a wide range of books and some old numbers of *Vogue*. I didn't see any family photographs anywhere; nor any of any other kind. The walls were decorated with framed reproductions. Not at all the sort of room belonging to an old lady, and a suburban widow at that. I must have misread the number on the gatepost and got the wrong house.

The wrong street even. What with the missing sign and the darkness, it was quite possible.

'So you must be Mademoiselle Gremet?' I called out nonchalantly.

'That's right,' she answered from the bathroom.

'Oh no you're not!' I laughed.

'Why ask, then?'

She now emerged, smiling, wearing the dress she'd taken out of the wardrobe and fresh silk stockings through which the marks of the ropes were still visible. A pair of high-heeled slippers showed off her dainty feet.

'You look very charming,' I ventured.

Back in the sitting-room she sat down on the sofa and I took a chair.

'I was expecting something like this,' she said. 'I should have given you the chance to get it off your chest in the Métro. It would have saved you a journey.'

'Is that why you left me so abruptly?'

'What do you mean?'

'Because you thought I was on the make?'

'Oh, did I get it wrong?' she said, pretending to be disappointed. 'There was I thinking it was my looks that were irresistible.'

'Don't worry,' I said, 'they are. But let's get down to business, shall we?'

'Good idea,' she said calmly. 'Then I might find out why you came to my house this evening. It's hardly the weather for going visiting.'

'Is that what you said to the other two?'

'They didn't give me time.'

'What happened?'

'What right have you to ask me questions?' she cried angrily. 'I don't see why I should put up with you any longer!'

'You'll have to until I've cleared up one or two things,' I said. 'You intrigue me.'

'If women had to answer questions from every man they intrigued, there'd be no end to it. Still, I suppose you did rescue me . . . But first of all there's something *I'd* like to know.'

'How I managed to turn up in the nick of time? That's easy. Chance. Pure chance. I was looking for a woman whose son was in the same POW camp as I was in Germany. I wanted to let her know he's all right. I was told she lived at 32, rue Jean-Jaurès. But I must have got the wrong house.'

'Very likely,' she said.

I couldn't tell whether her sarcasm was directed at my entire story, or simply at the bit about getting the wrong house.

'You want me to tell you what this is really all about?' she said, tracing the pattern on her dress with her broken nail. 'It's a put-up job, and not even a very original one. Every schoolboy dreams up the same thing. You meet me; you like the look of me; you try to engage me in conversation; I snub you. Don't worry, you're not the only one. Anyway, I don't know how you got hold of my address so quickly – congratulations – but you found it out somehow, and sent two of your pals on in front to put the frighteners on me. Then lo and behold, you appear at the critical moment, brandishing your revolver. Incidentally, that was very risky. There was another notice in today's paper reminding people what will happen to them if they're found carrying arms. Anyway, you foil the villains and save the heroine. All that's missing is the final kiss. I'm amazed you haven't claimed it yet.'

'Later,' I said. 'So you thought it was all put on, did you? And that's why you didn't fire?'

'Yes to both questions,' she said. 'I reserve judgement concerning the kiss.'

She said all this with a charming impishness. But as soon as she'd finished, her eyes lapsed into their former weariness.

'You're tired,' I said, getting up.

'Done in,' she admitted.

Her eyelids drooped and she lay back against the cushions, crumpling a newspaper as she did so.

'You'd better go,' she whispered. 'I need to be alone.'

'Not until I've found out certain things,' I said. 'And as far as the play-acting theory is concerned, you can forget it. I didn't know those two men, let alone set anything up with them. And they might be back.'

She didn't move. She just lay with one wax-pale hand on the newspaper. I took out my pouch and pipe and sat down again.

'It looks as if this is going to take some time,' I said. 'May I smoke?'

She assented with a vague wave of her hand. I filled my pipe carefully and held up the pouch.

'Like me to roll you a cigarette?'

'No, thanks. I don't smoke.'

I lit up, then said through a cloud of smoke:

'Tell me, how did those men— Oh, perhaps I should introduce myself. My name's Nestor Henry.'

She opened her eyes, sat up, and began toying absent-mindedly with the newspaper.

'I see,' she said. 'You want to know my name. It's Lydia, Lydia Daquin.'

'Well, Mademoiselle Daquin,' I said, 'how did these two men set about you? Don't worry – it's not just sadistic curiosity that makes me ask. I want to help you.'

'It all happened in the traditional manner. There was a

knock at the door. I asked who was there and a voice said
"Police". So I opened up, and there they stood with their
revolvers. They told me not to make any noise, or else.'

'Wait a minute,' I said. 'You say they were armed?'

'Yes. Both of them.'

'You're sure of that?'

'It's not something you make mistakes about.'

'And you didn't call for help?'

'With both of them pointing guns at me? I'm not that
heroic. Anyway, what good would it have done to scream?
This place is very isolated.'

'There's another house opposite.'

'The tenant's hardly ever there. So they pushed me in
here, tied me up and asked where I kept my money. I said
I hadn't got any, so they— my God, I think you did arrive
just in time . . . Maybe they would have tortured me!'

'And they hadn't been here long?'

'When you arrived?' she said. 'Not long at all. That's
why I thought it was a hoax.'

'Well, it wasn't. Not on my side, anyway. They must
have waited deliberately until it was dark.'

'I suppose so.'

For a while we didn't say anything. A piece of coal
collapsed in the stove. The wind shrieked around the house.
There was the dull thud of an explosion in the distance.
She started.

'Jumpy?' I said.

'A bit. What was it?'

'Gunfire, I think.'

'Oh! This awful war!' She put her head in her hands.

'It didn't seem to affect you so much this morning,' I
said.

'It's not the same in the daytime. I know it's idiotic, but
you don't feel so helpless when it's light. But at night—'

'I see what you mean. But that's not what I was getting at. You seemed pleased this morning that the bombs were falling nearby.'

She raised her head slowly, combing her fingers through her hair and then linking them together under her chin.

'Where did you get that idea from?'

'From watching your face. You can't deny you were pleased when someone said 103, rue Desnouettes might have been hit.'

She shook her head. There was a pale smile on her pretty lips.

'You make me sound very wicked.'

'Number 103 wasn't hit, as it happened. But something *did* go wrong there.'

'What do you mean?'

'Do you know a man called Briancourt?'

'No. Who is he?'

'A tenant at number 103. He was found dead.'

'Thanks to the famous bomb I wished on to the building – is that it?'

'No. I told you – the house wasn't hit. He was shot twice.'

She betrayed no emotion, but her eyes hardened and she said sharply:

'Why are you telling *me* this? What's it got to do with me?'

'Nothing, I hope. But might I ask what you were doing in the building?'

She sighed, then said with an attempt at lightness:

'Well, since I didn't throw you out, and since I've started to answer your questions, I might as well go on. You're good at asking riddles, and I can think of worse ways to pass the time.'

Her fatigue had now disappeared, if fatigue is the right

word for what made her droop visibly every so often: it
didn't look like ordinary weariness. Her vitality had now
revived as had her smile, though it was forced and sickly.
Her eyes betrayed a variety of feelings.

'You haven't answered my last question,' I reminded her
gently.

'Don't look so disapproving, Monsieur Henry. I'll tell
you everything. I wasn't doing anything particular at
number 103. It's got two entrances, and I was just using
the courtyard as a shortcut. I was in a hurry because of the
alert – I didn't want to stay too near the old Air Ministry
buildings . . . I think there are troops billeted there. I
thought I'd go across the river to Passy or La Muette. It's
less dangerous over there.'

'With bombs raining down all round you?' I said. 'That
doesn't make much sense.'

'No . . . Oh, I admit it was foolish. All in all I don't
wonder that policeman was so cross.'

I mumbled an answer through an ungracious yawn. It
made her yawn too.

'I'm going to make some coffee,' she said. 'No reason
for me to change my routine just because you're here.'

'I'd love a cup,' I said.

We went through into the kitchen and she dug a handful
of sweet-smelling grains out of a bag. She had some real
coffee hidden away, the little devil.

While she was preparing it I made a vague excuse and
wandered off into the other room, where I discreetly opened
a few drawers. They were all full of papers which were of
no interest to me and which I didn't have time to examine
anyway. One desk contained three 1000-franc notes that
even the most inexperienced thief couldn't have missed.
This seemed interesting, although I didn't quite know why.
Like a lot of things I'd seen and heard that evening.

I went back into the kitchen, where Lydia was pouring boiling water into the percolator, a *Fashion* cigarette between her lips.

'I thought you didn't smoke,' I said.

'One cigarette from time to time isn't smoking. Might I ask what you were looking for in there?'

'Photographs of possible rivals,' I said. 'I didn't find any, so there's still hope. Apparently you're free.'

She tapped the percolator a few times with a spoon.

'So you knew the building had two entrances,' I said.

She gave an exasperated sigh.

'Why can't you let me get the coffee ready in peace?'

I did so, and a few minutes later we were back in the sitting-room drinking it as if we were old friends. It tasted rather peculiar to me. But then I hadn't drunk real coffee since 1940.

I took up my questioning again between sips. Yes, she did know about the two entrances. To explain how she'd found out, she launched into a long story about artists. I asked her if she was one herself. No, she was a model. Had she lived in Bois-le-Roi long? Quite a long time, yes. Wasn't she afraid, all on her own? Tonight's incident proved she wasn't really safe living in such an isolated spot. Did she have a gun? With a wry laugh she said she hadn't. She didn't want to be put in front of a firing squad. And although she'd suspected a hoax just now, she was ready to admit that the real reason she hadn't used the revolver was that she wasn't familiar with the things and didn't even know how to fire one.

As she talked she picked up the newspaper that had been lying on the sofa and turned it over and over in her hands. My eyesight seemed to have become keener. I could read quite clearly *Nous, les Gosses* in small print under the heading CINEMA PROGRAMMES. The objects around me seemed unusually distinct, as if my sight was making some sort of supreme effort before failing entirely. And this impression wasn't far from the truth; everything suddenly went cloudy and my head felt unbearably heavy. I leaned my arm on the table, knocking over my coffee, and tried to stand. I felt as if I had a grand piano on my back.

The so-called Lydia Daquin had got up too. She'd retreated towards her bedroom and was standing leaning against the door, her hands outspread. She looked terrified, she was trembling, but there was a smile on her lips, a smile that was apprehensive but triumphant. She was at the end of her tether, panting with exhaustion.

She was only waiting for me to collapse to do the same herself.

I took a step towards her, but my shoes were made of lead, my temples buzzed and I had an irresistible desire to go to sleep.

'That's the second time . . . in one day . . . you've tricked me,' I gasped.

Then I fell down on the floor.

4 *Florimond feels*
  sorry for me

I came to lying on an uncomfortable bench in surroundings that I recognized even in my numbed state: a police station. There were even two coppers bending over me and almost brushing me with their moustaches. Without giving me time to gather my wits they began bombarding me with questions. What was I doing sleeping out of doors during the curfew? *And* in the rain? And why couldn't I wake up a bit? And so on. They were really het up.

The smaller of the two stuck a pistol under my nose, so to be on the safe side I put my hands up. But the larger cop shoved them down again and told me not to play the fool: he ate blokes like me for breakfast. Then his colleague started rattling off more questions.

'What were you doing with this in your pocket?'

I realized the pistol he was brandishing was mine.

'I've got a licence,' I said.

'Really?' he said sarcastically. 'Let's have a look.'

I reached for my inside pocket, where I kept my wallet. Gone.

'It's with my other papers,' I said.

'Oh, sure!' said the fat one. He'd have doubled up laughing if he'd been physically capable. 'But where *are* your other papers? When we found you on the path beside the railway line, all you had on you was your pipe, your tobacco pouch, six hundred-franc notes and the gun.'

'It's all coming back to me now,' I said. 'I was attacked. They must have—'

'That's right . . . They took everything except the gun and the money! A likely story!'

He was right. It didn't sound very plausible. Yet it was true, except for the fact that it wasn't some unknown pick-pocket but Lydia Daquin, or whatever her name was, who'd relieved me of my wallet and left the rest. Very strange behaviour, thought I.

'Listen,' I said. 'Wouldn't it be simpler if you checked with Paris? I'm a private detective and I *have* got a permit. My name's Nestor Burma.'

To my surprise this last piece of information didn't elicit a single cry of admiration, but as I was digesting my disappointment a third policeman, who'd so far been too busy reading the paper they'd found in my pocket to take any part in the proceedings, suddenly spoke.

'Hey, Sarge! Look at this!' he said. 'What does it mean?'

The sergeant pored over the crossword page.

'Faroux,' he read. 'Farouche Inspector Faroux.'

'What does it mean?' said the other one again.

'It means,' said the sergeant, 'that this fellow's an anarch-ist and spends all his time trying to undermine authority. You can see what his politics are from the dopey way he acts and the superior smirk on his face . . . Faroux's an Inspector in the CID . . . '

He then started to cudgel his brains, assisting the process by twisting his moustache and scratching his head. He could have done with a haircut. Finally he thought he saw the light.

'Well, I'll be damned,' he said, as much to himself as to the others. 'Don't you see? He must be mixed up in some case that Faroux's in charge of. I know Faroux quite well – I've even got his home number. I might just do him a good turn and ring him up – tell him I've got someone here calling himself . . . what is it? . . . Nestor Burma? Detective, my foot. There's something fishy here if you ask me.'

He went into the next room and came back ten minutes later rubbing his hands.

'I don't think we've been wasting our time,' he said smugly. 'Inspector Faroux told me to keep our friend here in solitary until he comes by tomorrow morning to question him.'

So they stuck me in a cell. It was only slightly dirtier than the other room, but less well heated and without any light at all. Before the door clanged shut I heard four o'clock strike, and the sergeant congratulating himself on having been right about me all along.

Florimond Faroux came at about ten, looking more like an undertaker than the real thing. After he'd told the local policemen he'd look after me from now on, we left the sinister building together.

We walked in silence for a little while, then he said:

'I've got a lot to tell you. I left you to stew in there for the rest of the night because, after yesterday, I didn't want you doing the disappearing trick on me again. Really, someone with your experience should have known that if I'd really wanted to nab you I wouldn't have telephoned you first.'

'I thought of that,' I lied. 'But as you had someone watching my office you could afford to, couldn't you?'

'I didn't put him there,' said Faroux, looking genuinely embarrassed. 'That was the others' idea. I don't know what you've done to them back at Headquarters, but you've been in their bad books for some time. They'll pin something on you the first chance they get.'

'You didn't come all the way out here to tell me that?'

'Among other things, yes. I also wanted to ask you a question.'

'Not more questions!' I said. 'Of course, you haven't asked me yet how I came to get taken in charge thirty miles from Paris at three o'clock in the morning. Don't tell me you've stopped keeping track of my movements!'

'There you go again,' said Faroux. 'You're never serious and you never give a straight answer. I'm not surprised they've got it in for you at HQ. I can't understand you: if a thing's black *I* can't bring myself to say it's white.'

'You're a funny kind of cop, then.'

'Yes. There's not many like me left, more's the pity. I can tell you, after you'd left the scene of the crime yesterday I wasn't very proud of the way I'd treated you. Especially when I saw how all the chaps back at the office were out to get you. I was so disgusted I said to myself: I'm going to warn him . . . tell him to stop behaving so mysteriously all the time . . . It can only get him into trouble. So I telephoned you, but as you weren't there I just left it. Then the next thing I knew, that sergeant was waking me up at half-past three in the morning! When I realized I'd got you pinned down I decided to let you spend a night in the cells, to teach you to be a bit less secretive.'

We'd come to a fork in the road, and the wind was howling all round us. We both shivered. Faroux turned up his coat collar.

'I didn't want to say all that in front of those coppers,' he said. 'And out here isn't much better. You don't know a quiet café, do you?'

I told him I'd booked a room near the station and didn't

have to give up my key until midday. So we set off for the bar in the square.

When we got there I was surprised and delighted to find that my wallet hadn't been stolen by the charming Lydia after all: I'd taken it out to check my identity card number when I was filling in the register, and in my haste to join Arthur must have dropped it instead of putting it safely back in my pocket. I didn't hear it fall because of the sawdust on the floor and the racket the customers in the bar were kicking up. They got tight as fast now on ersatz apéritifs as they used to do on the pre-war originals.

I thanked the barman, rewarded him for his honesty, and told some cock-and-bull story about why I hadn't used the room the night before. I said my friend and I were going upstairs to talk business and that if there was a bottle of white wine left on the premises we'd club together to pay for it.

'Now let's get down to some serious talking,' I said when we got upstairs. 'What's all this about regretting the way you behaved and warning me the CID are after me?'

Florimond Faroux sat down in an armchair that had seen better days.

'It's all because of that bloke yesterday,' he said.

'Briancourt?'

'So-called.'

'What do you mean?'

'His name's not Briancourt, it's—'

There was a knock on the door.

'Come in,' I said.

The barman appeared with a bottle and two glasses, put them down on the table and disappeared again.

'His name was really Barton,' the Inspector went on. 'Henri Barton. He belonged to the Alfred Thévenon gang – the one that carried out the famous train robbery in Le

Havre on 15 January 1938. And everyone at HQ thinks he was in touch with *you* lately.'

I whistled.

'That's the way the wind blows, is it? Where did they get that idea?'

'He had one of your agency cards tucked away in his wallet. "Nestor Burma, private investigator: surveillance, missing persons, discretion guaranteed" – you know the one. He could only have got it from your office. Anyhow, it doesn't really matter *how* he got hold of it. The fact is he did, and what's more you turned up in the building where he was killed. You have to admit it's a bit suspicious.'

'I was looking for the man who runs the bookshop,' I said.

'Tell them that if you like. They won't believe you.'

'Who's "they"?'

'Superintendent Martınot. And—'

'— and the rest of his squad, of which you're a part.'

'I don't share their views, but I'm the only one who doesn't. And now they've found an excuse for getting their hands on you, they'll take advantage of it. They're like a pack of hounds in full cry – I've never seen anything like it.'

'They don't really think I killed Barton, alias Briancourt, do they?'

'My dear Burma,' he sighed. 'If they had the slightest suspicion of that they'd have pulled you in long ago.'

'What do they believe, then?'

'That he hired you to work for him, and that it was a big enough job for you to take the trouble to visit him in person to report progress. They think the ten bank notes found in his room were to pay you with, and that you probably have a good idea about what happened, which is why you said you didn't recognize the body. Hence they reckon you could throw a lot of light on the killing if you felt like it, but you just won't cooperate.'

'They must be barmy!'

'You're the one who's barmy, doing everything you possibly can to confirm their suspicions. Do you think that supercilious air of yours does you any good? Or the way you shake off the tails we put on you and disappear? Martinot's theory is that Barton thought he was in danger, and hired you to find out who his enemies were and protect him from them. If you just told the police what you discussed with him when you met it could give them some useful clues. Why won't you?'

'Because I'm hand in glove with the killers, of course! It's very simple – listen. Barton offers me ten thousand francs to protect him. I go and tell his enemies what he's up to and they give me double to keep out of their way. Then I'm just on the way to Barton's place to tell him I'll stick with him for thirty unless the other dummies make me a better offer when I bump into you. The killers must have got there before me.'

'That's right – joke about it . . . Oh well, you're old enough to know what you ought to do if you know what's good for you.'

'Yes,' I said. 'And I'm going to tell you the truth.'

'The Burma version, of course,' he said. 'I don't want to hear any more of that. Well, I've warned you. Now it's up to you to decide whether to admit to knowing Barton or just go on playing the fool.'

He started to get up, but I stopped him.

'Listen,' I said. 'Believe me or not, as you like – it's all one to me. But I give you my word I never had anything to do with Barton or whatever his name is. I have no idea how my card came to be in his wallet. I haven't got any of them left in the office. They're pre-war stock and I haven't had any more printed since the agency reopened. But the thing is, this case interests me, because I'm involved in it now whether I like it or not. So tell me about Barton and the train robbery, and above all tell me what you think was frightening him.'

'The denunciation, for Heaven's sake! The anonymous letter!'

'Look,' I said, 'if I have to wring the information out of you drop by drop we'll be here to till tomorrow night! I'm not in the mood for guessing games, so tell me what happened, right from the beginning. It'll save me a visit to the library.'

'The papers were full of it at the time,' said Faroux suspiciously. 'It's a wonder you don't know all about it.'

'It does ring a faint bell. But if Barton was one of the gang, you must have been refreshing your memory lately. Come on, Faroux, spill it!'

He sighed.

'You always get round me somehow, don't you?'

He rolled a cigarette, emptied his glass, and stared so hard at the empty bottle I rang for the barman to bring us another. Then he lit his cigarette and began.

5 The train robbery

'On 15 January 1938 four masked bandits attacked a train waiting in a siding at Le Havre station. It was carrying a consignment of gold bullion on its way to the Bank of France. Four people were killed: two bank employees, a uniformed policeman and a plain-clothes inspector.

'I'll skip the technical details of the hold-up – it was incredibly daring – but they got only two crates of gold, which they loaded into two getaway cars. It was later discovered that the drivers of the cars didn't take part in the hold-up itself.

'A couple of hours later one of the cars ran into a roadblock just outside Rouen, and two of the occupants were arrested without putting up much resistance. The third managed to escape and hasn't been seen since. As far as we can discover he was a student without any family who'd never tangled with the law before, though he professed to be an "ideological bandit". He was known as Fernand Gonin. The two who were arrested were Louis Dargy and Maurice Vallier.

'One of the crates of gold was in the car, and it didn't take us long to recover the other, because that same night the second car was found crashed off the road near Saint-Germain-en-Laye. Inside was not only the gold but also one of the gang members, dead, with three bullet-holes in him. The slugs matched those from one of the pistols used on the train guards. We guessed, correctly as it turned out, that the death, and the accident, were the result of a violent disagreement between two of the gang. We hoped that the driver, who was obviously responsible for the killing, was injured himself and unable to get far. But although we searched the whole area there was no sign of him until the day he gave himself up. The crate carrying the gold had been smashed in the accident, and when the bars were counted four were found to be missing. He'd obviously made off with as much as he could carry.

'Both cars had been stolen so they were of no help to us, and as for the two fellows we'd arrested they were like a couple of clams. We were sure they were just the fall guys, and that one of the three still on the run was the brains behind the operation. We had a hunch it was the one who'd made off with the gold, but we knew nothing about him except that he was clever and had a lot of nerve. Not much to go on. Then, just when we didn't know which way to turn next, the CID got an anonymous letter revealing his name: Alfred Thévenon.

'We'd come across him before. He was a good-looking chap, a sharp dresser and a bit of a Don Juan. We'd already suspected him of some brilliant confidence tricks, but until now he'd always worked on his own and never been involved in violent crime. Yet his mentality was too similar to that of our man for there to be any doubt. The letter said we'd be able to nab him in the rue Stinville – out in the street – at three in the afternoon on 10 February. All we'd have to do was be on our toes!

'Now it so happened we knew the rue Stinville already, because a man called Barton, whom we'd been watching for a few days because we vaguely suspected him of being mixed up in the robbery, lived at number 13C. And it turned out that he *had* been involved. He hadn't done any of the shooting, but he was one of the two men waiting in the getaway cars. He insisted he wasn't present when the fatal argument took place near Saint-Germain, and that was true. Thévenon had dropped him off at a local railway station so as to settle whatever grudge he had against the other man. Anyway, that's neither here nor there . . . Let's get back to Barton. He sensed he was being watched and decided it would be best for him to denounce Thévenon in the hope of getting off more lightly if he were arrested himself. His plan worked. The two surviving killers, Thévenon and Vallier, were sentenced to death, Dargy to penal servitude, and Barton himself got seven years. He was sent to serve them in Caen.'

'Seven years!' I said. 'Then how—'

'Later,' said Faroux, taking a swig at his drink, which prompted me to do the same. 'I'll answer questions later. Now, where was I? Oh yes. The fact that Barton wanted us to pick up Thévenon in the street suggested two things—'

'That he had an appointment with him himself, but didn't know where he was actually holed up,' I said.

'Exactly. Oh, we'd have given a lot to know that ourselves. Because of the gold, you see? He must have stashed it away somewhere, and it can't have been far from his own hide-out. He hadn't set foot in his usual place on the boulevard Péreire since 14 January, and we had no way of finding out where he'd been since. When we questioned him later we did everything we could to get him to tell us. We gave him a good going over – I mean, a very thorough cross-examination – but he just laughed in our faces.'

'Did you find out in the end where he'd hidden himself and the gold?'

'No. But an idea struck me some time later. Supposing there wasn't a hiding place? – for the gold, I mean. Supposing it wasn't Thévenon but some passer-by who took it? Because when we first mentioned the four gold bars he was speechless with surprise. It was only later that he started talking and trying to lead us up the garden.'

Tobacco, wine and the interest of the story were beginning to stimulate my memory.

'You mentioned that one of the gang turned himself in,' I said. 'That was Thévenon, wasn't it? If I remember rightly, the snatch in the rue Stinville didn't come off.'

'No – some fool of a journalist nearly blew the whole thing,' said Faroux, going purple with anger at the very thought. 'We had it all set up, and one of the evening papers went and put a picture of Thévenon on the front page, with the caption, "The man who robbed the Bank of France". Someone from headquarters had leaked the information. So we had to change our tactics right away. We had all the ports and railway stations watched, and circulated photographs and descriptions of Thévenon everywhere. We even offered a reward. We'd as good as got him. He couldn't set foot out of doors without being recognized and arrested.

'He realized himself that the game was up. But then he did a most extraordinary thing. With the entire police force and half the civilian population of Paris after him, he treated himself to one last afternoon of freedom, going round and round the city in a taxi with the curtains drawn. The driver had recognized him, but couldn't do anything about it because he had a revolver stuck in the back of his neck.'

'Yes, the papers went to town about that, I remember. Thévenon wasn't the only passenger in the cab, was he?'

'No. He'd called a rank by phone and told the driver to go to what turned out to be an empty house. As soon as the taxi drew up there, Thévenon rushed out of the door and leapt inside.

'Twenty minutes later, in the Bois de Boulogne, they picked up a woman wearing a veil. She and Thévenon spent the afternoon in the back of the cab behaving as if it was a hotel bedroom. When he was too busy to keep the cabbie covered, she took over the gun. Hot stuff, that pair, if you ask me!

'Thévenon dropped the woman off early in the evening roughly where he'd picked her up, and told the driver to take him to 36, quai des Orfèvres. Police headquarters. The man couldn't believe his ears, but he did as he was told.

'And when Thévenon got inside the building he marched straight up to the head of the CID's office, dumped his pistol on the desk and said: "I've come to claim the reward. I'm giving myself up."'

'Quite a sensation!'

'He had nothing on him: no papers, no money. He'd given his last couple of thousand francs to the taxi-driver to keep quiet about the woman. But it was too good a story for the man to keep it to himself.'

'Yes, I remember,' I said. 'The business about the rear mirror! A lot of low-minded people got a laugh out of that!'

'We were convinced Thévenon had told the woman where he'd hidden the gold,' Faroux went on. 'So we tried to find her. But the taxi-driver couldn't tell us anything about her, and by the time we'd got together some photos to show him of the women Thévenon was known to have had dealings with, he'd been dead for a week – killed in a car crash.'

'Any signs of foul play?' I said.

'No. Just a run-of-the-mill accident . . . So there's the whole story.'

Faroux sounded relieved, as if he'd got an unpleasant job over and done with.

'Satisfied now?' he asked. 'I got quite carried away telling it all. An intriguing business. But you should have stopped me – you probably knew it all already . . . Anyway, Barton's dead now. It looks as if it was an underworld murder, probably to pay him back for grassing on Thévenon. And Martinot thinks that's just what he was hoping to avoid when he got in touch with you.'

There was a moment's silence. I stared at the curtains, trying to collect my thoughts. Our little journey into the past had brought us back full circle to 17 March 1942 and the murder in the rue Desnouettes. There were still a few things I wanted to know more about, but Florimond Faroux hadn't finished with me yet. I rang for the barman and ordered yet another bottle: he obviously thought we were a couple of abandoned soaks.

Then the conversation, or rather monologue, started up again. Faroux told me how in June 1940 Barton and some other prisoners from Caen were being transferred to another gaol when their train was bombed. It was thought that Barton had been killed, but he must have been among the handful of convicts who took advantage of the chaos to escape. This explained how he'd come to be in Paris lately, savouring Occupation turnips instead of prison porridge.

Soon after his escape from the train, however, Barton had been caught by the Germans and sent to a POW camp. But when he was repatriated and demobbed via Marseilles he gave the authorities a fictional account of his past.

As far as the present investigation was concerned, the police had made up their minds: they set it down as a gang killing. The only thing they were still doubtful about was my own involvement.

Their theory hinged on several details. First, no one in

the building had heard the shots, so unless all the other inhabitants were either deaf or accomplices to the murder the gun was probably fired during the air raid, which indicated that the killer or killers must have been uncommonly cold and calculating. This timing was corroborated by the fact that Barton wasn't fully dressed: suffering from a hangover, he hadn't bothered to move when the alert sounded, but when the bombing began he'd started getting ready to go down to the shelter and been interrupted by the killer. This cool customer, with every opportunity to help himself to the ten thousand francs on the table and the notes in Barton's pockets, had left the money untouched. Thus the only plausible motive was a powerful desire for revenge.

'We've no doubt that the killer's a gangster,' said Faroux, 'and we'll get him sooner or later. But it'd be sooner if you'd talk. I believe you when you say you didn't know Barton, despite the fact that he had your card. But Martinot won't.'

He shrugged.

'Well, I suppose you know what's best for you. I just wanted to warn you that they're out to get you, that's all. Now it's up to you.'

6 *Q.E.D.*

When Faroux had left I called the agency.

Hélène gave such an enormous sigh when she heard my voice I thought she must be in the arms of some admirer. But it was just relief. She'd been worrying about me all this time, and she had news – some good, some bad.

She told me the bad news first. The police had searched both my flat and the agency that morning. The good news was that we had five new cases on our books. I said I didn't have time for them now and told her to get Reboul to deal with them. If they were too much for him she'd have to hire an extra hand.

Then she told me a man called Chambot or Chabrot, she hadn't quite caught his name, had left the office only a couple of minutes before. He'd been very disappointed to find I wasn't in, refused to tell her what he wanted, but said he'd call back in the evening. When I asked what he looked like she said he was fat and well dressed. Probably another client. Things were really looking up.

I told her not to worry any more, and said I'd look in at the office either that evening or the next morning. Then I added a few insults about the police just in case the line was being tapped, and hung up.

I wasn't very hungry, but having installed myself in a

quiet corner of the bar I ordered a snack. As I chewed I thought of Lydia Daquin. She'd obviously made up the name on the spur of the moment, and I remembered now that before doing so she'd glanced at the newspaper she was holding. There'd been an advertisement in it for the film *Nous, les Gosses*. Of course! Daquin was the name of the director. It may also have caught her eye because it resembled the name of the famous designer, Paquin. Perhaps she hadn't been lying when she said she worked in the fashion business. I pondered over some other questions, both professional and personal, concerning her, but all *that* did was bring on the beginnings of a splitting headache, so I gave it up.

Instead I left the hotel and set off to do what I'd originally meant to do before I'd been so strangely distracted: I went to see Madame Gremet.

It turned out that, as I'd suspected, I'd overshot the rue Jean-Jaurès on my first attempt, and turned instead into the next street, l'Allée du Platane or Plane-tree Lane, doubtless so called because of the chestnut tree on the corner. No wonder I hadn't seen the name: the sign was hidden by branches.

When I got to 32, rue Jean-Jaurès I found the old lady at home and reassured her about her son. Then I described Lydia Daquin and asked Madame Gremet if she knew anyone like her living in the next street. She said she didn't, so I left and went and had a look at the house where so much had taken place the night before. It was as quiet as the grave, with the shutters and gate closed and no smoke coming from the chimney. The luscious Lydia must have left the nest as soon as her nocturnal exploits were over. Not surprising. That's why I hadn't bothered to come back before.

Someone in the house opposite who thought he was all

alone was torturing his accordion. I soon put a stop to that by ringing the bell. A peculiar-looking chap of indeterminate age opened one of the windows a crack and cautiously asked me what I wanted. I said did he know the name of the girl who lived over the road, but he said he didn't. He could give me the name and address of her landlord, though: Armand Jander, 4 rue Albert-Blain.

'You didn't hear anything unusual last night, did you?' I said.

'No.'

'Yes, you did,' I said. 'A car driving off and a bloke shouting.'

At that he closed the window and disappeared. But he didn't go back to his accordion. I must have frightened his muse.

Needless to say the rue Albert-Blain was right at the other end of Bois-le-Roi. When I got there I was led in to see Monsieur Jander by a woman who'd probably once been his housekeeper and had since become his wife.

A man of about fifty was sitting reading in front of a cheerful fire and stroking a kitten that was lying on his lap. He had a bald patch only partially hidden by the kind of skull-cap you see only on the covers of pulp novels. But his appearance was as attractive as the accordion-player's had been repellent, especially as he was smoking a pipe.

'Sorry to bother you,' I said, 'but it's very urgent. I need to speak to your tenant in l'Allée du Platane about a legacy. She's going to have quite a surprise. Do you know where she is?'

'Oh, has Mademoiselle Verbois come into some money?' he said.

'Yes. About two million francs. From a relative on her mother's side I don't think she even knows about. He died in the middle of the exodus in 1940 and we've been looking for the lucky beneficiary ever since. Why?' I smiled. 'Is the young lady behind with her rent?'

M. Jander glared at me and threw up his hands in protest. 'What ever do you mean, young man?' he said. 'She's been my tenant since the autumn of 1941, and she's always paid on the dot! I'm just pleased for her, that's all – she's a nice person, even if she isn't easy to get to know. But there's nothing wrong with being independent.'

'No. But it doesn't make our job any easier,' I sighed. 'Can you tell me where she is today so I can give her the news?'

He dropped his hands back on his lap, and the kitten shot out of the room.

'No. She has to go to Paris for her work sometimes, but I don't know where.'

He was giving me some very curious looks.

'I hope she really is the person I'm looking for,' I said. 'She *is* the Mademoiselle Verbois who works for a fashion house, isn't she?'

'That's right. She's a real artist, and gets well paid for it too. I'm afraid I don't know who she works for, though.'

'Never mind,' I said. 'I'd have liked to give her the good news myself, but as that's impossible I'll have to get her to come in and see us. I'll drop a note into her letter-box. Thank you for your help.'

'It's a pleasure,' he said, still staring at me. Then he pointed. 'That's a very fine pipe you've got there, young man,' he observed. 'I've been wanting to mention it since you came in. Is it an ox head?'

'A bull,' I said. 'I bought it for sixty francs in '39. Now it's worth five hundred.'

'Everything's going up,' he said. 'Does it smoke well? It looks as if it might be a bit heavy.'

'Not at all,' I said, and we launched into a lengthy conversation about pipes and tobacco, on which he was something of an expert. I admired his collection, and when he found out that I always carried more than one pipe on me he was really impressed, comparing me favourably with the young slickers who weren't really serious about smoking and only did it because they thought it was smart . . .

I left the house with his compliments ringing in my ears, satisfied that I'd learned Lydia Daquin's real name.

A little later I caught a train to Paris that got me in at six o'clock.

I called in at my flat to change, and found it in chaos after the police search. Just as I was about to change my suit I noticed some rust marks on the trouser leg which suggested I'd been transported to the spot where the police found me in some kind of barrow. So Lydia Verbois had managed to dispose of me all on her own.

After I'd changed I made my way to the office. Hélène was all agog, but before I satisfied her curiosity I asked how she'd been managing with the new cases. She said Reboul couldn't cope with them all and didn't know anyone who could help, so she'd put an advertisement in the paper. It was murder trying to find staff, and so on and so forth . . .

When we'd got that out of the way she told me about the police search. Apparently Martinot and his men hadn't found what they were looking for and had gone off empty-handed. He'd left a man behind to keep watch in the street in case the building flew away. So at least one of them had been earning his salary – until three o'clock, that is, when he'd either got fed up or been called off. Perhaps Martinot had given up hope of my returning to the fold, and decided to change tactics.

I was just about to bring Hélène up to date on my own adventures when there was a long, impatient ring on the bell.

'What's this, another client?' I said. 'If it goes on like this we won't know what to do with all the cash.'

'It may be the chap who came in this morning. Chambrot, Cabot, or whatever his name is.'

'Go and see, will you?' I said. 'And if it's him, tell him I'm out.'

Hélène was soon back again carrying two cards of different sizes.

'It *is* him,' she said. 'Chabrot. Emmanuel Chabrot. He insists on seeing you. He asked me to give you these.'

On the smaller card was printed: Emmanuel Chabrot, Director Q.E.D. On the larger one the following curious message was elegantly typed: 'Never say you're out when Q.E.D. calls. What Q.E.D. says counts.'

I toyed with this missive for a moment or two and raised my eyebrows at Hélène, who was waiting expectantly.

'Send him in,' I said. 'I'll try not to let him hear my knees knocking.'

Monsieur Chabrot was a stout man of about fifty, rather in the style of Louis XIV. He may have been furious at being kept waiting, but he wasn't letting it show. He had removed his hat – a bowler which he held between kid-gloved fingers – revealing a receding hairline that lent him a certain impressiveness. His eyes were hard, and beneath the left one was the mark left by a monocle. I offered him a seat, and he set his hat down on my desk.

Evening was drawing in. I asked Hélène to put on the ceiling light and then said briskly:

'What can I do for you, Monsieur Chabrot?'

'I'm the director of Q.E.D.' he said grandly.

'What does that stand for?'

He gave an irritated laugh.

'Come, come, Monsieur Burma. You don't mean to tell me you've never heard of Q.E.D. – the smallest paper with the biggest stories?'

'Oh, that!' I said. 'Is that what you've come about?'

'Not exactly.'

'What then?'

'You.'

'Me?'

'Yes. If you're Nestor Burma, the private detective.'

'I am. What about it?'

Emmanuel Chabrot pulled out a monocle, polished it on a silk handkerchief and screwed it into his left eye. Then he tilted his head so that the lens caught the light, and directed it upon Hélène.

'I should like to talk to you in private,' he said.

'I have no secrets from Mademoiselle Chatelain,' I replied.

'That's as may be,' he said. 'But perhaps I have.'

'In that case,' I said, starting to get up, 'there's no point in continuing this discussion.'

He raised one hand soothingly.

'Now, now! What a fiery fellow you are!' he murmured. 'My word, yes. Just the kind of man I'm after. But at the risk of seeming a boor I repeat that I should like to speak with you alone. After all, there's nothing to stop you repeating our conversation to Mademoiselle when I've gone – I've nothing against it. It's just that I don't like talking business in front of a third person.'

'Oh, you're shy, are you? You should have said so in the first place,' I said sarcastically. 'Actually I'm a bit of a cynic myself. You interest me, Monsieur Chabrot.'

'I hope you'll be even more interested when we've had a talk. I'm no ordinary client.'

'I can see that,' I said. 'Hélène, would you mind going through to your office?'

'And now, Monsieur Chabrot,' I went on when she'd gone, 'I'm all ears. Please be brief.'

He slipped his hand inside his overcoat and brought out an expensive-looking cigar which he proceeded to light with a showy gold lighter. Then he leaned towards me.

'How much are you prepared to pay for top quality information?'

'What about?'

'You.'

'Nothing,' I said. 'I know all there is to know about myself. Besides, I'm broke.'

'Everyone is these days. At least so they say. But business goes on as usual. That's why I'm here.'

'What do you have in mind?'

His plump face leaned even further forward, and a pungent wisp of smoke wreathed itself round his monocle.

'In my job I'm obliged to rub shoulders with people from all walks of life. All walks . . . And I just happened – Bless you!'

I'd sneezed. The rain from the day before was having its effect.

'I just happened,' he went on, withdrawing his face to a more normal distance, 'to find out something about you. You have a lot of enemies, Monsieur Burma, and they're plotting against you.'

He paused, drew himself up and adjusted his monocle.

'Have you heard of "La Petite Roquette?"'

'Yes,' I said. 'It's the prison for women.'

'It is now. But what about several years ago? In 1926, for example?'

'It was a detention centre for young delinquents.'

'What a charming euphemism. And in cell eleven, division ten—'

'Third floor,' I said.

'Ah!' he exclaimed. 'I can see we're going to get along. You know the place, then?'

'Yes. Quite well.'

'And you wouldn't by any chance know the young offender who was in that cell from 15 February until 14 July of that year, would you?'

'As well as I know myself,' I said. 'Was that all you came about?'

He shook his bullet head so that his monocle glinted, and a large piece of ash fell from his cigar on to his overcoat. He brushed it away fussily with his sausage-like fingers.

'The fact that we both know about this little incident is of no importance. But it might be better if your enemies didn't find out about it. It's just the sort of information they'd use against you.'

'There's nothing wrong with a few months in prison,' I said. 'Especially at that age. It's called sowing your wild oats.'

'Certainly. But people might start to have doubts if they heard that the head of a detective agency discovered his vocation while he was locked up in a cell.'

'It'd be good publicity, that's all.'

'It might also encourage the authorities to keep a closer eye on his activities – perhaps even shut down his agency altogether. You'll have heard of the new regulations concerning your profession?'

'The police already know about the little incident you refer to,' I said. 'So your threat's an empty one.'

'Let me tell you a true story. A few years ago a man shot a politician. He was tried and sentenced to death, but in the meanwhile the victim survived and so the sentence was commuted. The man was sent to prison, but let out seven years later on condition that he never returned to Paris. He did come back, though, but the police turned a blind eye until a certain newspaper mentioned the fact and they were obliged to make him leave.'

'I knew about that,' I said.

'I know. I just wanted to remind you.'

'And have you got a newspaper in mind now?'

'I am the director of Q.E.D.'

'Do you mean to say that rag still exists?' I said disgustedly.

He took out his cigar to give me the full benefit of his commiserating smile.

'Come, come, Monsieur Burma,' he said. 'I know a wind of virtue has been sweeping the country since 1940: no more dancehalls, no more Pernod. There's even talk of a social revolution. But I won't insult you by thinking you believe in all that poppycock.'

'I'm not *that* stupid, no,' I said.

'Good. Even if we do have publication difficulties sometimes these days, there are other ways of spreading information. Virtue may be fashionable, but so is the anonymous letter. Everyone's busy denouncing his neighbours to one police force or another. You may have been too busy tracking down unfaithful wives to notice, but there's a foreign power occupying our country. Its police force is very touchy about certain things, and might be afraid someone like you could go back to his old ways. They could easily put you away in a safe place if they thought you were dangerous. After a few months they'd probably realize you were harmless and let you go again, and then you'd be able to take advantage of the publicity. Still, it would be very unpleasant while it lasted.'

'Especially as I'm a Jew,' I said.

'You've got quite a sense of humour, haven't you?' he said with a laugh. 'But I'll bear in mind what you say.'

'Don't bother,' I said. 'How much do you want?'

He stubbed out the remains of his cigar.

'I'm going to surprise you now, Monsieur Burma,' he said. 'I don't want anything.'

'Don't tell me you're a philanthropist!'

'Exactly! And since you look as if you're coming down with a cold, I'd be glad to see you go and stay somewhere healthier for a while.'

'Can you be more precise?'

He hadn't leaned forward for some time, but it was more than he could do to stop himself now. He looked as if he was stretching out his neck ready for the guillotine. Very apt.

'I won't beat about the bush,' he said. 'I know I don't have to with you. Here's what I want you to do to buy my silence. Someone I do business with intends to seek your services. I want you to refuse. And to make quite sure your professional curiosity doesn't get the better of you, I want you to be elsewhere when this person calls. How about a few days on the Côte d'Azur? It'll soon be spring. Just the thing to head off that flu before it lays you low.'

'I wish it was the only thing likely to do that,' I said. 'Will you pay my fare?'

He laughed.

'That's rather a lot to ask. Perhaps I could make a small contribution.'

'I do love Paris in the spring,' I said. 'The women are so beautiful.'

'There are no women in gaol,' he said drily.

I cleaned out my pipe and said nothing.

'Well, what do you make of my proposition?' he said.

'I'll think it over.'

'Don't take too long.'

'In a hurry, are you?'

'Very much so.'

'No more than I am,' I said. 'I'm the electricity board's worst customer, Monsieur Q.E.D. – I'm so quick I generate my own. I've been itching to throw you out ever since you walked in, but first I wanted to hear what you had to say. Now I've heard I'm going to give myself that pleasure.'

I got up, walked round the desk and reached Chabrot just as he stood up himself. We were the same height, and I was so close to him when I spoke that his monocle misted over.

'You've been trying to scare me for the last quarter of an hour. It's about time I showed you what I'm made of. Forget your little game and let me get on with my job – if you don't I'll stuff your monocle right down your slimy throat! Now scram!'

Hat in one hand, gloves in the other, he backed towards the door.

'I'm sorry we haven't been able to keep our conversation within the bounds of politeness—'

'Hop it!' I said. 'You'd better get writing if you want your letter to get there by tomorrow. But don't bother to send a copy to the Gestapo. I've been Germany's secret weapon for the last ten years. My real name's Adolf Hitler.'

'You can't resist a joke, can you,' he hissed, 'no matter what it may cost you! . . . I'll give you twenty-four hours. Tomorrow evening I'll telephone this office, and if anyone's still here I shall carry out my threat.'

'You'll get an answer from the Fiat Lux Agency whenever you call,' I said. 'An answer you won't forget.'

He shrugged his shoulders and left.

7 *A chat*

Hélène stood looking at the door through which our visitor had disappeared, slamming it behind him. Then she gave a whistle and turned to me with a sardonic gleam in her eye.

'What was it Marc Covet sent you to get yesterday morning – tobacco or gun-powder? It certainly seems to have hotted things up.'

'Quite,' I said. 'That bloke wanted to blackmail me. Amusing, don't you think?'

'Very. Two police searches and a visit from a crook all on one day – it's hysterical!'

I put my hand on her shoulder.

'No need to get worked up, Hélène.'

'If only I knew what it was all about,' she sighed.

'I was just going to explain when Q.E.D. interrupted. I'll soon put that right, but first let me cast my eye over the cases that have come in since yesterday. The one that Chabrot wants me to refuse might be among them, unless he was just making it up to frighten me out of Paris.'

Hélène handed me the files. Nothing out of the ordinary. I gave them back, she put them away in a drawer, and then made it clear she required a detailed account of my adventures.

She listened in silence, not showing any surprise – we'd been working together too long for that. The only exception ever was the time when I took a break in Barbizon and not one person died in my arms. On that occasion she'd seriously wondered whether I oughtn't to retire.

When I'd finished my narrative she said nothing at first – merely drew pensive patterns with one finger on the top of my desk. Very irritating. Then:

'So you don't buy the revenge theory?'

'Yes and no.'

'What does that mean?'

'I don't believe it was a settling of old scores. I suspect it was another kind of revenge. But I'm not even sure of that. You see, Thévenon was a loner, and the hold-up in Le Havre was the only time he'd ever worked with a gang or been involved in violence. I can't help wondering what made him change his ways. But it's too soon yet to answer that question. Anyway, there isn't really anyone left who's likely to have wanted to punish Barton for betraying Thévenon. Vallier's dead – executed – and Dargy's doing a stint of hard labour. That only leaves Gonin, and though Barton revealed his name, nothing else has emerged about him. So he wouldn't be so stupid as to attract attention by coming out into the open to pay Barton back.'

'So, all in all, the only person with a motive was Thévenon?'

'Yes. But he's dead. And though ghosts may go around in shrouds and chains, I've never heard of them wielding revolvers.'

Nor had Hélène.

'But even if Thévenon can't be our man, someone close to him could. Someone who loved him so much they couldn't get over his death and took the first opportunity to avenge it.'

'The mysterious woman in the cab?'

'Exactly. When she went on the famous taxi-ride she must have known about Thévenon's past, so she's bound to have loved him very much. What do you think, Hélène? Women understand these things better than men.'

She looked up at me with troubled grey eyes.

'Yes,' she said quietly. 'I'd have to love someone very much to do a thing like that . . . Or else feel very sorry for him.'

I snapped my fingers.

'Of course! Pity! That's what it was! By the time she came to that last rendezvous and got into the taxi with him she'd already stopped loving him. She just felt sorry for him. You've just put paid to the revenge theory, Hélène! And if she didn't love him she wouldn't have bothered to avenge his death three years later. There must be some other motive, and I think I know what it is. Do you?'

Hélène hesitated a second.

'The gold?'

'Yes.'

'But did Thévenon really go off with it? There's never been any proof. And the theory of a casual passer-by is just as plausible.'

'It's like the theory of the gang murder,' I said. 'Very convenient . . . Personally, I'm convinced Thévenon did take a cut of the swag, and that's why Barton's dead, why the girl's scared, and why people like the Sloper, the boxer and Monsieur Q.E.D. are getting so excited. Don't ask me yet exactly how they all fit in to the story – there are still some things I don't know.'

'Aren't you the man who can K.O. any mystery?'

'I'm the only one who's been K.O.'d so far,' I said. 'But I'll soon put that right. In the last twenty-four hours everyone's been playing ducks and drakes with me. A girl shakes me off in the Métro and then drugs me . . . I'm tricked by a spiv, then locked up by the cops . . . The CID and a blackmailer are after my blood . . . It's time I went on the offensive. For a start, how did Barton get hold of my card? Who did we use to leave them with before the war? – we haven't had any printed since then.'

'Thomas Cook's and various other travel agencies . . . '

'Well, he couldn't have got it from there!'

There was a silence, broken only by the sputtering of my pipe.

'I wonder why Barton ratted on the leader of the gang,' I mused.

'Aren't you satisfied with the official explanation?'

'Not entirely.'

'But Barton *did* get away with a minimal sentence.'

'There must have been another reason as well,' I insisted.

'I know!' she said. 'Barton and Thévenon must have stayed in touch, perhaps seen one another, while Thévenon was in hiding. That's how it was possible for the police to set the trap in the rue Stinville.'

'I see what you mean. You think Barton knew where the gold was hidden, so when he realized he was going to be caught he thought he'd win a light sentence by turning over his boss, then, as soon as he was let out, go and pick up the gold.'

'Yes.'

'You're forgetting Thévenon was very tight-lipped, and Barton probably didn't know where he was holed up. Otherwise, since Barton knew he himself was suspect, he wouldn't have taken the risk of arranging the snatch practically on his own doorstep. In any case, when Thévenon found out Barton had split on him, do you think he'd have just kept quiet and let him walk off with the loot? *I* don't think so! He'd rather have told the police where the gold was hidden.'

'True,' she said. 'Unless—'

'What?'

'Unless Barton and the woman in the taxi *both* knew where the gold was, and both hoped to pick it up. As Thévenon had avoided involving her up till then, he may have been afraid to try to foil Barton by telling the police, in case they went straight to the spot and caught the woman instead.'

'That makes sense,' I said. 'But I reckon taking the four bars of gold was really just a bit of bravado, and no one else knew anything about it, whatever the police may think. I even wonder whether there *is* a hiding place, or whether the gold isn't lying at the bottom of some river.'

'In which case you can't expect to get much out of all this.'

'No, but I can't help being involved. I'm in it up to the neck whether I like it or not. Partly because of that card, and partly for other reasons.'

'What other reasons?'

'Oh, never mind.'

'I've got it!' she said, slapping her forehead. 'Not your other mysterious reasons – the card! I've just remembered – I found a packet of them in a drawer when we reopened the agency, and gave them to your friend Fred Lecomte, the barman in the rue Daunou. I thought some of his clients might become ours some day. I'd completely forgotten about it.'

'My God!' I said, jumping up. 'Fred's got his wits about him – he's sure to be able to help us. I'll go round and see him straight away. I could do with a drink.'

'Me too,' said Hélène.

8 Light at the end of the tunnel

Fred's the only barman I know who wears glasses. It makes him look like a harmless intellectual. But his cocktails are far from harmless.

When we arrived at L'Ile de la Tortue he was scribbling on the back of one of my cards. He looked up. We sat down on two high stools.

'Have you given one of those cards to anyone lately?' I asked.

His eyes sparkled shrewdly behind his glasses.

'You're the second person who's asked me that today,' he said.

'Who was the first?'

'A bloke in a felt hat.'

'A copper?'

'Yes.'

'What did he want?'

'Well, there I was doing some sums on the back of one of your cards – sorry about that, but paper's hard to get hold of – there I was, just like I am now, with a pencil in my hand, luckily for me – you'll see why in a minute . . . And this fellow walks in, and I say to myself: "This'll be good." He's not one of my regulars but he smells as though he's had a drop, even though this is a non-alcoholic day.

So I say: "No need to show me your badge." And he looks furious – fit to be tied. Then he laughs, picks up the card, turns it over and says: "Have you got many like this?" "About fifty," I say, and show them to him.'

Here Fred turned round, drew aside the sinister black flag with a skull on it that hung from one of the shelves, and opened a little box to show us, too. Then he went on with his story.

'"What do you use them for?" he asks. "For writing down what my customers owe me," I say. "Do you give credit?" he says, as though he's really interested. "To people I know," I say meaningly. Then he asks me if I know a man called Briancourt, if I've given him a card, and if so why, etc. And I say yes – I gave it to him to put down the score at poker. Well, that unleashed a flood of questions. Did Briancourt come in often? Quite often, I said. Since when? Just the last few days – never before that. Was he alone? Yes – the people he played with were regulars he'd met here. Were any of them in at the moment? No. Had he ever received any telephone calls here? I didn't think so. Could I explain why he had my telephone number in his address book then? That was just the kind of stupid question I was waiting for. I pretended to play it straight. "Listen, Inspector," I said. "You know the way the things are. I won't try to beat about the bush. Briancourt used to call me from time to time to find out if I had any so-called English cigarettes. That's how I knew his name and how he knew my number." It went down a treat – chatting to him like that, man to man. It was written all over his face. And what's more, everything I'd said was true. That *was* how I found out Briancourt's name. He asked two or three other questions as he was leaving, took one of the cards, and said I'd probably be called on to give evidence. Then he went off back to police headquarters as happy as a sandboy.'

Fred stopped, grinning from ear to ear. Then he poured himself a vermouth and lit a so-called English cigarette, waiting to be congratulated. I obliged.

He accepted my tribute modestly, then leaned forward across the bar and spoke in a low voice, wafting wreaths of smoke in my face.

'I'd read in the paper that someone called Briancourt had been killed. When the copper came in and mentioned the name I realized it must be the same one. There didn't seem any point in mixing you up in it.'

'You made the right decision,' I said. 'Why did you *really* give Briancourt my card?'

'Because he was looking for something or somebody and couldn't find them. He was here the day before yesterday, looking terrible, as if it was the end of the world. "Things not going too well?" I said. Then he asked me if I knew any real private detectives. "You know what I mean by 'real'," he said, and gave me a wink. "And discreet into the bargain." I slipped him your card and said he wouldn't find anyone as good in the whole of Paris. He put the card in his wallet, finished his drink and left. I said to myself if he went straight to your place he'd draw a blank. It was a quarter past twelve and you'd be at lunch. I went off duty myself at one, and when I came back on at six Briancourt was already back here. He was full of the joys of spring, and had obviously put back a fair amount. He insisted on buying me a drink. "Thanks for the tip," he said. "That mate of yours, the detective, works miracles." He had something to eat here and left quite late, as tight as a coot.'

We went to another place for dinner. The prices at the Ile de la Tortue were higher than the regulations allowed and beyond my means. Over the dessert we tried to make sense of what information we possessed, and Hélène explained her theory, based on the hypothesis that both Barton and the woman in the taxi knew where the gold was hidden.

'Thévenon kept quiet when he was questioned because he thought the woman was the person most likely to get to the hiding-place first. Barton was inside, and wouldn't be out again for some time whatever happened. And that's just how it turned out. The woman picked up the swag, and when Barton got back to Paris he realized what had happened and set out to find her. That's why he was looking for a "real" detective. He was just about to hand things over to you when he bumped into her himself. Then there must have been some sort of a bust-up which ended in Barton's death.'

'Right there and then?' I joked.

'They might have arranged to meet the following day,' she said impatiently. 'Then some friends of Barton's heard of his death and went to the girl's place to get their own back. That's when you turned up.'

'So Lydia Verbois is the killer?'

'Yes.'

'And she's the woman in the taxi.'

'Yes.'

'Judging by the precautions she took to avoid being recognized, I'd guess the woman in the taxi was married and had some social standing,' I said. 'She can't have been just a young girl or she wouldn't have kept quiet about it afterwards. Either she'd have been frightened and the people around her would have noticed, or she'd have boasted about what she'd done. But Lydia Verbois is still young even now, three years later. And what's more, while Barton was being cured of his hangover yesterday morning, Lydia was with me in the air-raid shelter.'

'How do they know the exact time of his death?'

'No one in the building heard the shots, so they could only have been fired during the air raid.'

'What about while the sirens were sounding?'

'They wouldn't have been loud enough. And the siren nearest the house didn't start up until Lydia was already out in the street.'

'She seemed scared of the police, anyway,' said Hélène doggedly.

'I'll grant you that,' I said. 'I noticed it at least three times. First when she only went to the shelter to avoid being arrested. Then the way she got rid of me when she thought I was following her in the Métro. And then at Bois-le-Roi, when the men who'd attacked her had gone and she saw I had no intention of leaving, the way she disposed of me again, instead of simply calling the cops.'

'You see!' said Hélène.

'Yes, I see. And if the counsel for the prosecution is looking for further evidence, Lydia Verbois was afraid of drawing attention to herself by making too much noise. She didn't scream when "the Sloper" and his mate burst in. She didn't even shoot at them when she had the chance. She said it was because the house was so isolated no one would have heard, but the man living opposite was bound to have been at home – he obviously isn't the kind to go out much. But none of this proves anything. I ran away from the police yesterday myself, and I hadn't killed anyone! Lots of people are afraid of the police these days, for all kinds of reasons. It's not the same old force we used to know before the war. The Germans have introduced their Gestapo, as Monsieur Q.E.D. could tell you. You haven't mentioned him, incidentally. Where does he fit into your theory?'

She shrugged.

'Monsieur Q.E.D. seems very anxious to get me out of Paris,' I said. 'His story about wanting to prevent me taking on another client was just bluff.'

Emmanuel Chabrot didn't seem to interest Hélène much. Perhaps because she couldn't work him into her theory. But she clung to that theory none the less, and droned on and on about the girl.

'Tomorrow I want you to go reconnoitring,' I said, interrupting her. 'Try every fashion house there is and find out where she works. I hope I've described her sufficiently – I'm sorry I can't give you a photograph, but there weren't any in the drawers I searched.'

'Oh!' said she. 'So you went through her things, did you? Just to make sure everything was nice and tidy, I suppose.'

'I was looking for a revolver, if you really want to know.'

'So you agree she might have—'

'No,' I said. 'Just habit. She isn't anything like what you imagine. If you'd only seen her—'

'I get it,' she mocked. 'She's the other reason you don't want to give up the case. She seems to have made quite an impression on you.'

'I don't deny it.'

'And that's why you won't consider the possibility that she might be guilty.'

'That's why I'm sorry she's not,' I laughed.

'What?'

'That surprises you, doesn't it? You see, I know I'm not irresistibly attractive, so think how it would improve my chances if I had proof that she was a murderess!'

'Nestor Burma, you're the limit!' said Hélène indignantly.

Hélène went home to bed and I phoned directory enquiries from a café to ask for the number of Mademoiselle Verbois,

85

32 allée du Platane, Bois-le-Roi. I said I'd already looked in the directory and she wasn't there. They told me the number was Bois-le-Roi 3-95. I tried to call it but there was no reply. I wasn't really surprised.

Out I went into the cold dark streets, deserted except for French policemen and German soldiers on guard at the white barriers round cinemas and hotels. It was spitting with rain. I pulled my hat down over my eyes, turned up my overcoat collar and lit my pipe. Then I stuck my hands in my pockets and started walking. My brain works best when I'm on the move.

Lydia Verbois might have been afraid of making too much noise, but she wasn't the only one. The two thugs who attacked her could have used their guns after the situation swung in their favour, but they did nothing of the kind. They just ran away.

My imagination set to work on this, and arrived at a theory which, if it didn't succeed in removing the veil altogether, at least managed to lift a corner of it.

And that wasn't all that was lifted. A violent gust of wind almost whipped my hat off, and I realized I was standing on a bridge: the Pont au Change. On the other side, massed forbiddingly against the sombre sky, stood the Conciergerie.

I had an idea.

Thanks to what Fred had told Faroux I hadn't been followed since that afternoon. I'd no need to be afraid of the police now, at least until Monsieur Q.E.D. carried out his threats. And as there was no reason for the cops to suppose I knew anything about their interview with Fred, I could go just like any other member of the public and demand to know what they meant by searching my flat. I might pick up some information.

By now it was nearly eleven o'clock, but I knew Martinot's reputation for keenness. Rumour had it that he slept in his office. There was a good chance he might still be there.

9 The midget

Commissaire Hervé Martinot was sitting chewing a matchstick and staring into space, but he soon came down to earth in order to haul me over the coals. I bore it with my usual stoicism.

He explained why he'd ordered the two searches, why he'd put a tail on me and why he'd taken it off, and why he regarded me as an undesirable character. In his opinion there were too many people like me allowed to run loose. Private detectives were riff-raff, operating on the fringes of legality and treating the police like dirt. Any government worth its salt would get rid of them at a stroke—

Here he waved his arms and sent the inkstand crashing into the telephone.

He took a deep breath. Since I had the nerve to come and ask for explanations in the middle of the night, he'd be only too happy to tell me what he thought of me. If I wanted his opinion there were too many . . . And so on.

There was more chance of the war being over by Christmas than of getting any information out of this nut. So I just let myself be thrown out, thankful he didn't have me locked up.

When I got to the top of the stairs, not feeling very proud of myself, I found Florimond Faroux coming up with one of his colleagues. Between them was a small boy. There was something comical about this threesome that cheered me up at once.

'What's this?' I said. 'Playing nursemaid now? Or have you been put in charge of catching truants? You ought to be ashamed of yourself, terrorizing little children like that – he should have been tucked up in bed long ago!'

'This child could be your older brother,' said the Inspector. 'He's nearly forty.'

'Good God! Is he Little Tich?'

'His double. Mac from the Médrano Circus. We picked him up after the show.'

I bent down and looked more closely. The midget tossed his head in a grotesque gesture of defiance: the feeble yellow glare from the blacked-out lights showed a misshapen face, still bearing traces of make-up, with an enormous pair of bulging, furiously malevolent eyes.

As I came close to him I caught a powerful whiff of perfume.

'What are you doing here at this time of night?' said Faroux.

I pressed the second button of his overcoat as though it was a bell.

'Curious as ever, I see,' I said. 'Don't tell anyone, but I'm an outraged citizen and I came here to wreak my vengeance on Superintendent Martinot. The trouble is he's too thick-skinned. I'm going home to sharpen my knife.'

'Don't take any notice,' said Faroux to his goggling colleague. 'His mind's gone.'

They went off down the gloomy corridor.

Faroux's comment might come in useful if ever I appeared in court!

I continued on my way down the stairs, but before I'd

got far I stopped dead, thought for a moment, then turned and went quickly up again.

I'd remembered that Barton had been shot in the stomach. And the bullets had been fired by someone much shorter than he was . . .

I asked the Inspector on duty, who was enclosed in a kind of glass box, if he thought Faroux would be long. He shrugged. I said I'd wait, and sat down on a bench whose imitation leather seat had been dented by generations of backsides, guilty and innocent alike. I puffed nervously at my pipe. My mind was racing.

After a time a door opened and Florimond appeared, alone, outlined against the light from within. As soon as he'd shut the door I went up and grabbed him by the arm.

'You again!' he said angrily.

I dragged him out of earshot of the glass cage.

'Don't be so bad-tempered,' I said. 'You know I told you the truth about the card you found on Barton. But I'm still interested in the case, anyway. Tell me about the midget.'

I was right. He'd been brought in for questioning, and though he hadn't yet been charged with the murder he probably would be before long. The police had been going through their files and come up with Mac, whom Thévenon had once felt sorry for and taken under his wing. Mac had been eternally grateful, and it was only a small step from that to the conclusion that he had avenged his idol's death. The more so as the ten thousand francs they'd found on Barton's bedside table reeked of the scent the midget made such liberal use of, and had probably come out of his pocket.

Faroux burst out laughing when he saw the expression on my face. He threw in a bit of American folklore.

When Chicago gangsters executed one of their men for treachery, it was their custom to leave a silver dollar on the body – an allusion to the thirty pieces of silver for which Judas betrayed Christ. The midget had probably intended the same kind of symbol.

'Ten thousand francs is a lot of money,' I said. 'A hundred would have done just as well.'

'He probably wanted the amount to be proportionate to the gravity of the crime,' said Faroux. 'Anyway, all these misfits are round the bend.'

'Even so,' I said, 'ten thousand francs! How could he afford it?'

'He must have scraped it together somehow – borrowed a bit here and a bit there. It was in one-hundred- and five-hundred-franc notes.'

'So you've got the killer.'

'Don't put words into my mouth. We're working on the idea, that's all. But there's plenty to back it up – the perfume, and the fact that Mac's just the right height. Unless of course the murderer was of normal height and knelt down to do the shooting!'

He chuckled. 'That's the sort of theory that should appeal to you!'

'I'll think about it,' I said. 'Have you found the murder weapon?'

'If we had we wouldn't be bothering with details. But we didn't find so much as a water pistol at the midget's place. Anyway,' said Faroux, who'd started fidgeting, 'it's time you went and got some sleep.'

'I get it,' I said. 'You're the second person to throw me out of here tonight. I mustn't outstay my welcome. Goodbye. You'll find what you need at the end of the corridor.'

By the time I got to the rue Fontaine I'd been stopped four

times to show my *Ausweis*. Twice by the French and twice by the German police. I dived into the first place I saw that was 'Open from ten till dawn'.

Twelve pretty girls whose scanty attire had nothing to do with the clothing shortage were flaunting themselves, as advertised, in time to some languorous music. A delightful spectacle, but I hadn't come here to enjoy myself. After downing half of the drink I'd ordered at the bar, I went to the phone and called up Jo Debeckar, an athlete friend of mine. The bell rang for some time at the other end, but finally there was an answer.

'Hello, Jojo,' I said. 'Nestor Burma here. Still working at the Médrano?'

'Is that what you woke me up to find out?' he growled.

'No. To ask you if you know a midget called Mac.'

'Mac Guffine?'

'Maybe. Is he Irish?'

Jo's laugh almost shattered the receiver.

'I'll say! He was born Dubois in the fourteenth arrondissement.'

'Can you give me his address?'

'Do you want to hire him? He'd be ideal for tailing someone if you put him on stilts.'

'Actually I intend to hide him in a lady's bra to gather secret information.'

'He'd love that. Just up his street.'

'What *is* his street?'

'Just a second.'

After at least eight he came back on again.

'Ringers' Hotel,' he said. 'In the rue de la Tour-d'Auvergne.'

The street was dark enough, but Ringers' Hotel looked even darker. The door was shut, so I gave a peremptory ring on the night bell. The night porter was obviously a heavy sleeper. I used the wait to dent my hat in the authentic style.

'Police,' I said as he opened the door. I held up a red, white and blue card that was anything but authentic, and mumbled something about having to make a final check on Lofty Mac Guffine's room.

'What a job,' I said. 'Never a minute's peace.'

'If you hate the job as much as all that,' he said, yawning, 'why don't you do something else and leave the poor little beggar alone?'

He told me where the room was and gave me the key. Then shuffled back to bed, showing no inclination to come with me.

When I entered the midget's room I was almost knocked over by the smell. There were three scent bottles on the shelf over the wash-basin, two empty and the third half full. It was called *Last Night*, and was made by Mirey in the rue de la Paix.

The walls were covered with photographs stuck up with drawing pins. On the floor lay a couple of suitcases that Faroux and his men had obviously emptied and then repacked any old how. I went through them again on my own account, but found nothing. A table drawer contained old programmes, stationery, and a bunch of publicity photos. It also held some other pictures, of the kind usually described as indecent, though I've never understood why. There were stacks of copies of *La Vie Parisienne* and *Sex-Appeal* in the wardrobe.

The smiles that looked down on the poor fellow's frustrated slumbers all belonged to female film stars. No men. Ever since Jojo Debeckar skimmed through an article on psychoanalysis in the dentist's waiting room he saw complexes everywhere. But maybe he wasn't far wrong this time. Mac must have been painfully aware of his physical disadvantages.

I took three particularly interesting photographs down from the wall, and found a fourth in a folder on the bedside table.

The first three were the work of professionals, though the names had been removed when the photos were cut out. The fourth had been taken by an amateur – by the midget himself, to judge from the camera angle. And the two people in the picture were clearly unaware of his presence.

The woman could be seen quite clearly, but all you could see of the man was his chin.

Although the clothes she was wearing varied, all four pictures were of the same woman. Lydia Verbois.

I put the photos in my pocket and went home to bed.

10 Death at the wheel

I went to sleep with a throbbing head, sneezed several times during the night, and woke up with flu. Monsieur Chabrot *would* be pleased.

While I was getting dressed it struck me that Faroux had omitted certain details when he told me about the train robbery. Deliberately or otherwise he hadn't mentioned the midget or other people who'd had connections with Thévenon. I'd have to pay a visit to the National Library and take a look at what the papers had said about the case at the time.

A quarter of an hour later I was in the Métro, wedged between an overweight housewife and a weedy fellow with glasses. The weed had got hold of a newspaper. I peered at it over his shoulder.

The day before there'd been just a few lines about the discovery of Barton's alias Briancourt's body. Today this paper at least was more generous, and in an article on the front page reminded its readers of the 1938 hold-up. By glancing over some more shoulders I saw that all the papers were now taking an interest in Barton's and Thévenon's exploit.

Before I went into the library I dropped in at Firmin's, the café in the rue des Petits-Champs.

One of the customers, previously engaged in shooting a line to Mademoiselle Marguerite behind the bar, turned round as I said good morning to the assembled company. He had bags under his eyes and at the knees of his trousers, and his nose was radiant for reasons that had nothing to do with the weather. It was my reporter friend, Marc Covet. He asked me if I'd got what I wanted at the address he gave me. I said I had, but that I'd be economizing on tobacco as I had flu. Then I tried to order a grog, but Mademoiselle Marguerite wouldn't bend the rules for me, so I had to make do with an ersatz coffee and two lumps of real sugar.

There was a newspaper lying damply on the bar, so I had a look at it while Marc went on playing the alcoholic Don Juan. There was a long piece on the Barton affair.

'Your colleagues are certainly going to town over this,' I said to Marc.

'Pah!' said Marc contemptuously. 'They're just beginners. They weren't around when things were really humming.'

'I haven't been able to get hold of the *Crépu*,' I said, 'but I suppose you must have done a spread on this too?'

'Not a thing,' he said. 'I left it to the office boy. Still, if I really wanted to I could put all their noses out of joint. I assure you, my dear Burma, I—' He checked himself. 'Odd that you've brought the conversation round to this subject, isn't it? You wouldn't have a personal interest in it, would you?'

'Not specially.'

His watery eyes narrowed, then he laughed, showing that it's possible to get by without toothpaste, but it doesn't do your teeth much good.

'You can stop looking so conspiratorial,' he said. 'It won't wash. You've kept me with my tongue hanging out for information often enough in the past. But now I'm my own man again, at least as far as this case is concerned. As I was saying, if I wanted to do an article on it I'd leave these youngsters standing. It's my baby, this one – I know all about it.'

'Very lyrical,' I said. 'I always thought you must have Mediterranean blood. But if you ask me it's just hot air.'

'I get it,' he said, laughing. 'You're trying to pump me. Right, I'm more altruistic than you are – offer me the right sort of drink and we can do business.'

'A coffee?' I said.

'You must be joking, or else the flu's affected your mind. Let's go into the back room. It's darker there. The alcohol might come out of hiding.'

A minute later Marc and I were in a secluded corner and he was telling what he knew.

Differences of style apart, his version of events was much the same as Faroux's. But as there were certain questions I didn't really want to ask, I began to regret having to fork out for the drinks.

I did learn one thing, though it was only of secondary importance. Covet was the newspaperman who'd jumped the gun by leaking Thévenon's photograph, and forced the police to abandon their trap. It was because Marc had sources of information at police headquarters that he prided himself on being so much in the know.

'A fascinating case,' I observed for want of anything better to say as Marc knocked back his fifth glass of calvados.

'You're telling me. And then there was that business about the gun.'

'What gun?'

'The revolver that was sent through the post.'

'Who to?'

'The cops. I'm the only reporter who knows about it. It was kept strictly under wraps. But, as I said, I had eyes and ears in the places that mattered. It didn't do me much good, mark you – I couldn't publish it. Since that first article of mine had almost blown everything, I'd had to toe the line.'

'So?' I said.

Marc kept me in suspense long enough for me to order a sixth round and then started up again.

'The revolver Thévenon threw down so theatrically on the desk at police HQ had only recently been bought and never fired. So it couldn't have been used on the train guards. (Of the ten bullets removed from their bodies, three had come from Vallier's gun, and seven from another weapon, previously believed to be Thévenon's, that hadn't yet been traced.) But a few days after he gave himself up, the CID received a parcel containing a Webley 7.35 which the experts identified as the weapon used in the hold-up at Le Havre. Apparently Thévenon was amazed when they showed it to him, but then burst out laughing and said something about some people being too clever by half. But he wouldn't explain what he meant. All he'd say was that the gun was his.'

'Who sent it?'

'Either someone Thévenon had left it with and who decided it was too hot to handle, or someone with a score to settle. Anyway, whoever it was he didn't have a police record.'

'Did they trace him?'

'No. He's still on the loose.'

'Then I don't see how you can be sure he didn't have a record.'

Marc Covet sighed.

'My dear gumshoe! The person who sent the gun didn't

bother to remove his finger prints. An old lag would hardly
have omitted to do that. Especially as one of his dabs is
very distinctive – it's got a scar in the shape of a cross on
it. They tried to match it in the files, but they couldn't . . .
The makings of a very good article, all that, don't you
think?'

'Sure,' I said. 'Was there a midget mixed up in it anywhere?'

'Mac Guffine, you mean? I was the one who found *him*,
too. I tracked him down to the circus he was working in
as an acrobat at the time. But he's not a crook. He was just
a friend of Thévenon's – very attached to him. A few hours
before Thévenon was executed, Mac burst into tears, then
slipped and fell in the middle of his act. He was seriously
injured. Rather a sad story, eh?'

'Is he very highly strung?'

'Yes and no. You have to be pretty cool to do an act like
his.'

'What would you say if someone told you it was Mac
who killed Barton?'

'If that someone was Nestor Burma I'd tell him he must
know something I didn't know, and that he was a secretive
devil. But it's not such a bad idea. Mac did make some
vague threats after Thévenon was turned in, though we
only laughed about it at the time. You can imagine the
stupid bets we made about "the mad midget!"'

But by now it was high time I went on to the library.

The periodicals room only confirmed my view that
journalists are unaccountable creatures. One of them went
into ecstasies about the visit to Paris of Conchita Moralès,
Hollywood's latest and hottest star, saying that nothing
short of Chicago-style gang warfare could add spice to life
now she'd gone. But the same newshawk was reticence
itself when it came to interviewing Barton's wife. Personally

I was far less interested in the colour of Conchita's cami-knickers than I was in the fact that Barton had a wife at all.

There was a photograph of her in one of the papers, but it was very blurred. The article said she was a brunette called Jeanne, who hadn't known anything about her husband's criminal activities. She'd been seriously ill a few months before, and the revelation of his guilt had threatened to bring on a relapse. Her own honesty was in no doubt, so the police didn't bother her, and the press gradually forgot her altogether.

The owner of one of the stolen getaway cars, an architect named Bouchot who lived in the avenue du Parc-des-Princes, was treated with similar discretion. The *Crépu*, well informed as usual, did once mention his name, but then followed the example of the other papers and ignored him. The owner of the other car, however, a doctor called Acker, got the full treatment. They almost gave details of his surgery hours.

I spent some time going through back numbers of *Q.E.D.*, but there was no mention of Emmanuel Chabrot. *Crime and Police* confirmed what Faroux and Covet had said about the midget, and also gave the name of Barton's lawyer: Lévy. With a name like that I'd be lucky to find *him* still in residence.

I made my way back to the agency at about midday and found Reboul laboriously typing out his report. He was only using one hand. He'd lost the other one earlier in the war.

We exchanged pleasantries and I asked him whether the advertisement for an assistant had come out yet.

'Yes – look!' he said laughing. 'The *Journal de Paris* put it in twice – once in the right place, and once on the front page, smack in the middle of the piece about the train robbery that's so badly printed you can't make head or tail of it. I hope they won't charge you twice.'

I had a look at the paper, and he was right.

'Where's Hélène?' I said.

'Don't know.' Reboul had started pecking at the typewriter again.

I flicked through the street directory and found Barton's old address: 13, rue Stinville. It was on the phone. Now I knew he'd been married I had to follow it up.

When I called the number, someone with his mouth full and an Auvergne accent answered. Obviously the concierge.

'I'd like some information about one of your ex-tenants,' I said. 'A man called Barton.'

'Not again,' growled the voice. 'Why the hell can't you leave us in peace?'

'You watch your language!' I bellowed. 'This is the police. You'd better tell me what you know about him.'

He swallowed hastily and became more accommodating.

'Well, er, not much. I never knew him myself. I've only been here since 1940.'

'Why did you say "Not again" when I asked about him?'

'Because someone called a few days ago to find out whether Madame Barton still lived here. I said I'd never heard of her, but the man insisted. So I told him I'd only been here since 1940 like I just told you. But he obviously didn't believe me, because he came round to see for himself. He kept on looking at the names on the letter-boxes. I just kept on saying I didn't know her.'

'What did he look like?'

He gave me a brief description.

'He wasn't wearing bright yellow shoes by any chance, was he?' I said.

'Yes, he was. I noticed them, even in the blackout. I remember saying to myself: "I'd like some like that—"'

'Blackout?' I said. 'Did he come at night then?'

'In the evening.'

'Just after he phoned, or some time later?'

'Oh, a few hours later.'

'What day was it?'

'Last Friday, I think.'

I thanked him and hung up.

Just at that moment Hélène came in through the door, all dressed up.

'I found your girlfriend,' she said. 'I was going to leave you a note. I didn't know you'd be here.'

'You were quick,' I said. 'What did you find out?'

'First let me congratulate you on your taste. And apologize. She looks as much like a killer as you look like a saint.'

'We just don't see eye to eye any more,' I said, laughing. 'When you see white I see black. And when you decide it was black after all, I've already decided it was white. Anyway, fire away.'

Hélène seemed rather lost for words.

'Well, Lydia Verbois—' she began.

'That is her real name, is it?'

'Yes. She works as a dress designer for *Irma et Denise* in the rue de la Paix, but she doesn't go in every day. She *was* there today though. I was lucky. It was almost twelve by the time I located her, so I waited until she finished work and followed her. She went to the Komak restaurant in the rue du 4-Septembre. She'll still be there if you're quick.'

'I will be,' I said. I scribbled a few lines on a scrap of paper. 'Give that to Covet. Tell him I'll get in touch for the answers later on today.' Then I hurried downstairs.

I'd hardly set foot outside the building when a car shot out of the rue de Gramont, swerved out of control and crashed into a tree. A policeman came running up and a group of onlookers gathered on the pavement. I joined them just as the policeman opened the car door. Inside, a fat, slightly balding man sat with his cheek against the steering wheel and his arms hanging loosely at his sides. There was blood on his hands, on his elegant pale trousers, and on the floor and upholstery of the car. Under his left eye, standing out against the livid cheek, was a white semi-circular mark.

11 *Lydia lies*

I made it back up the three flights of stairs in record time. Hélène had kindly replaced Reboul at the Underwood and he was dictating his report.

'Leave that for now,' I told him. 'There's a bloke dead in his car outside. Someone seems to have decided to use him for target practice. Go down and pick up as much information as you can. Hang around as long as you need to.'

Reboul was used to this kind of thing. He just said 'Right', adjusted the angle of his hat and grabbed his coat off the peg as he went through the door.

'What goes on?' asked Hélène.

'The director of *Q.E.D.* is no more,' I said. 'He'll soon be pushing up daisies. They've done him in.'

'You mean it's him in the—'

I nodded.

'Things are hotting up,' she said.

'Not for him. Someone decided to cool him off for good.'

'Did you see what happened?'

'I didn't need to. It's as clear as daylight. The Sloper, the boxer and Chabrot were all in the same gang – let's call them "The Gold-Diggers". The other two must have been waiting for Chabrot out at Bois-le-Roi the day before yesterday. That's why the door wasn't locked. They ran away to warn him I'd turned up – the Sloper must have seen me somewhere before. Chabrot obviously wasn't very bright and thought it would be a good idea to try and do a deal with me. One of his mates must have taken exception and shot him. But he was tough, old Chabrot – he didn't give up the ghost right away, and I'll bet you a war bond to a ration card he was on his way here to pour his heart out to me. Still, I can't say I'm sorry he died before he got here. I can do without having my office turned into a morgue.'

'Me too.' Hélène gave a little shudder. 'And the CID's shown enough interest in you as it is. Anyway, tell me who killed him? Was it the Sloper?'

'No. He's not up to anything as drastic as that. Whoever killed our friend the blackmailer wouldn't have given me time to introduce myself if we'd met the other night out in Bois-le-Roi.'

'So now there's another mystery man?'

'Listen, sweetheart,' I whispered, leaning forward. 'Just between you and me—'

Then I caught sight of her watch and straightened up.

'I must go.'

I found a seat in the corner of the restaurant where I couldn't be seen but had a good view of the rest of the room. I told the waitress I was in a hurry and ordered the menu advertised outside at 18 francs 50. That wiped the smile off her ruddy face. Then I paid in advance, left a hefty tip, which brought the smile back again, and started to chew the slice of blotting paper they called pâté.

Lydia Verbois was sitting with her back to me, but I could see her in a mirror. She was sharing a table with another girl and a charming-looking, slightly effeminate young man. They seemed to know each other well.

The young man ordered three coffees just as the waitress put some vegetables down in front of me. More blotting paper. But I gave the cook the benefit of the doubt, and put the lack of flavour down to my flu.

The young man now produced a packet of cigarettes and offered them round. The other girl took one but Lydia Verbois declined. They drank their coffees, asked for the bill, paid it and got up to leave. This was not exactly what I'd planned, but as soon as the door closed behind them I abandoned my lunch and followed.

To my relief they parted company outside. The other two set off in the direction of the Opéra, while the lady I was after strode away towards the Bourse. Her shoulder-bag had the initials L and V on it.

I quickened my pace to catch up with her. As soon as I spoke she turned round and went as pale as death. I had my pipe in my mouth, though I couldn't taste or smell the tobacco, and now I kept it clenched there and gave a knowing laugh. Like the ones I'd seen detectives give in films.

'My dear Mademoiselle Daquin,' I began.

'What do you want?' she said, recovering slightly.

'Just a chat.'

'Be quick then. I'm in a hurry.'

'I'll decide how quick I'll be.'

'I don't think so.'

I smiled.

'What's come over you in the last couple of days? You used to seem so sure of yourself. Aren't you afraid of attracting attention any more? Though I admit it wouldn't suit me either if you took it into your head to call a policeman, like that one on duty over there. Still, he must be bored. Why don't you shout for help and provide him with a bit of distraction?'

'What do you want?' she said again. She looked tired suddenly, and her voice had gone flat.

'To continue the conversation we began the other night. But the street's hardly the place for it. Come to my office – it's just round the corner. We can stroll there arm in arm like lovers. Then you won't be able to leave me high and dry again – Mademoiselle Verbois.'

She started when she heard her real name, but put up no resistance as I took her arm. We walked on in silence. Gradually the lightness went out of her step: she seemed to become resigned.

She stumbled once or twice going up the stairs to my office, and when she saw the plate on the door she stopped and tried to back away.

'Where are you taking me?' she said.

I laughed and told her what I did to earn my living. Then we went inside.

'Oh, good afternoon, Mademoiselle Verbois!' Hélène blurted out when she saw us. The girl's eyes widened, then she said lightly:

'You were at *Irma et Denise* this morning, weren't you?'

'Yes,' said Hélène. 'All part of the job. I hope you won't hold it against me.'

I put a stop to these polite exchanges by asking Hélène in my most professional manner whether she had any news of Marc or Reboul. She told me Marc couldn't get away from the paper before the evening, and Reboul was still hunting for information. I ushered Lydia into my office.

She seemed quite at ease answering my first few questions, which put me off a bit. But she did eventually say:

'What do you want to *know*?'

'The same as I did before,' I said with a sigh. 'Why you were in such a hurry to leave a building where a man was about to be killed. Why you rather hoped a bomb had destroyed it. Why two thugs came to your house and attacked you. And why you drugged me.'

'That's a lot of questions all at once,' she said.

'Not really. I've got plenty of others up my sleeve. But these will do to be going on with.'

'What right have you got to question me at all?'

'I'm a detective.'

'A private detective.'

'I'm not ashamed to admit it. If you don't want me to question you, perhaps you'd prefer a real policeman to do it.'

'That's not what I meant,' she said quickly. 'I was just thinking aloud. Did someone hire you to question me?'

'Possibly.'

'Yes or no?'

'If you answer my questions with more questions we'll never get anywhere,' I said. 'My answer is "possibly". I suppose you've heard of confidentiality.'

She laughed.

'Confidentiality's one thing, distorting the truth is another. And that's what you've been exposed to. I couldn't make out why you were so insistent the other night, but now I know who you are it all makes sense.'

She enumerated all the things she thought might have excited my professional curiosity.

'But you've been making a mountain out of a molehill,' she said finally.

'Possibly.'

Her eyes narrowed under their thick lashes.

'I hope you'll think what I'm going to say now is possibly true as well,' she whispered, 'and then let me go. I thought you wanted to press your attentions on me the other night.' And she proceeded to spin the same yarn as she'd served up at Bois-le-Roi.

'That doesn't explain why you drugged me,' I said when I'd heard her out.

'I thought a detective would understand that much! I didn't want you staying the night, that's all. How else does a woman get rid of someone in that situation?'

'By picking up the telephone. You could have locked yourself in your bedroom and called the police ten times by the time I'd broken down the door.'

'I prefer to look after myself,' she said tartly.

'Are you an anarchist then?'

'Possibly.'

'That would explain a lot of things,' I said.

'Some, perhaps – yes.'

'But not the way you left your house and didn't go back. Is that what you do every time an admirer gets over-insistent?'

She didn't answer for a moment.

'I lost my nerve a bit. I thought the two men might come back, and I was afraid I might have given you too strong a dose as well. I went and stayed with a girlfriend of mine.'

'The man who was killed in the building you say you only took a shortcut through wasn't just anyone,' I said slowly. 'His name wasn't Briancourt any more than yours is Daquin, or mine's Henry. His real name was Barton. You must have seen it in the papers.'

'What if I did? You see mysteries everywhere, Monsieur Nestor Burma. The connections you're trying to make are ludicrous! Why should I be interested in what the papers say? I've told you the truth and I'm not changing my story. And now may I go?'

'Not for a moment,' I said. 'Someone else was killed barely two hours ago. I don't know where or why, but I do know he's dead. His name was Emmanuel Chabrot, and he specialized in blackmail. He ran a libellous rag called *Q.E.D.* Does the name mean anything to you?'

'Nothing at all. May I go now?'

'One last thing. Have you ever seen this before?'

I leaned across the desk and showed her the snapshot I'd found in Mac Guffine's room. For a second I saw panic written on her face.

'No,' she said. 'I've never seen it before.'

'What I should have said was: "Is this a photo of you?"'

'It's of someone who looks like me.'

'Have you got a sister?'

She stood up.

'I don't wish to continue this conversation, if you don't mind,' she said, smoothing her skirt. 'It's gone on too long already, but I was taught never to contradict lunatics! I don't think you can keep me here by force, but if you try I'll have to go against my principles and call the police.'

She said all this in one breath, with a mixture of aggressiveness and desperation, as if she wanted to convince herself it was true. All the same, I could see from the look in her eye I wasn't going to get any more out of her. And maybe she *was* rash enough to shout for help.

'I can't keep you here, it's true, Mademoiselle,' I said. 'But I assure you I've got plenty more questions to ask you, and if I thought it was worth while asking them you'd see I know more than you think. Then you might change your attitude. But never mind – we'll carry on next time we meet.'

'I shouldn't bank on it,' she said. 'I've told you everything I know.'

'You've told me nothing. But I'm patient. Like a Red Indian. I used to read about them when I was a boy.'

After I heard Lydia close the outer door behind her I

went and gave Hélène a dressing-down about her unprofessional conduct.

'If you hadn't been so welcoming I'm certain she'd have told fewer lies,' I said.

'So she's a liar, is she?'

'Yes. But not a very good one. The only time she told the truth was when she said she'd never heard of *Q.E.D.* The name Chabrot really didn't ring a bell. It was pathetic to see how relieved she was to be able to give a straight answer for once.'

'Still, she's very attractive,' Hélène mused.

I laughed.

'You're telling me!'

12 Some clues

I went back into my office, opened the window and leaned out.

Lydia Verbois was coming out of the building. She was looking pensive. She took a few steps as though she was walking in her sleep, then made a lightning movement and a cigarette flowered between her lips. She drew on it two or three times, still lost in thought, then stopped and seemed to come back down to earth. She must have realized that with the tobacco shortage it was sheer provocation to smoke outside. She threw the cigarette away, and a tramp who was shuffling miserably up the boulevard scuttled over and picked it up while she disappeared into the crowd.

I closed the window again and, sniffing hard, began filling my pipe. It was a good way of checking on the progress of my cold. As soon as I lit up I realized it was making giant strides: the tobacco had no taste at all. So I abandoned the operation, just as a lugubrious incantation went up all over Paris: another air-raid warning.

I whipped out my revolver, and as the nearest siren sounded fired into the ceiling and threw myself on to the floor.

I heard Hélène shriek and the door burst open, and she

rushed over to where I was getting up, laughing all over my face.

'You fool!' she said. 'You frightened the life out of me!'

'I wanted to find out if it's possible to hear a shot and a body falling once the orchestra's started up,' I said. 'What were you doing out there?'

'Typing.'

'And the door's quite thick. So my experiment proved its point.'

'It looks like it – yes.' She was still quite shaken, but tried to cover it up by an air of efficiency. 'You haven't called Covet yet.'

'I want to talk to Faroux first,' I said. 'Call the CID, will you?'

A few seconds later Faroux's voice was on the line.

'Hallo,' I said. 'Is that the Chamber of Horrors? How's your most recent acquisition getting on?'

'If you'd only talk normally . . . ,' he said.

'All right. How's the midget?'

'He's all right.'

'You're still holding him, are you?'

'More so than ever.'

'Why? Has anything new come up?'

'You bet! It was clever of me to remember he'd made threats after Thévenon died. He's confessed.'

'What!'

'Yes. To everything. Surprised, eh? Well, Nestor Burma's not the only one who finds out whodunnit.'

'I hope you didn't beat him to death to get it out of him.'

'Of course not. We hardly touched him.'

'You're joking! You mean he told you all this of his own free will?'

'No. First of all he didn't seem to know what we were

talking about, but when he saw the weight of our argument he cracked.'

'Weight of your argument,' I laughed. 'That's a nice way of putting it.'

'Don't jump to conclusions,' said Faroux calmly: he really was pleased with himself. 'I mean that when we produced the bank notes and pointed out that a few minutes in his pocket would make them reek of the scent he uses, he came clean and confessed he was guilty.'

'Did he go into detail?'

'He's doing so now.'

'Would you be a pal and arrange for me to see him? Without saying anything about it to Martinot, of course.'

'Get to the point,' said Faroux. 'Why do you want to see him?'

'I've got some tips for him about how to grow taller.'

Faroux burst out laughing.

'I should have expected that! Well, we'll see.'

But he didn't seem wild about the idea.

'I'm no longer a suspect,' I pointed out.

'I know,' he said, without much enthusiasm. So I tried a new tack.

'By the way,' I said, 'some chap was found murdered outside my office this afternoon. You don't think I had anything to do with that, do you?'

'Don't be ridiculous,' he growled.

I promised him I wouldn't, and he said my voice sounded funny. I told him languishing in a clammy cell in Bois-le-Roi was responsible for that, and he recommended some unpronounceable inhaler. Then he hung up.

I called the *Crépuscule* and found Marc still there.

'What's got you all worked up?' he began.

'I'll tell you later. Have you got the information?'

'Easy. All it took was an hour in the files.'

'Get on with it then. I'm in a hurry.'

'Right. Well, the cars were both stolen, one from a doctor called André Acker and the other from an architect called Julien Bourguet.'

'Bourguet or Bousquet?'

'Oh, you've been going through our back numbers too, have you? That was a printing error. His real name was Bourguet. I remember because it was the same name as my current girlfriend's.'

'Your colleagues didn't mention him often enough to repeat the error.'

'You noticed that too, did you? I don't know why I'm telling you all this – you know as much as I do.'

'Tell me about Bourguet,' I said. Like Lucienne Boyer singing 'Speak to me of love'.

'As soon as he saw the article he came rushing round saying he didn't want his family name associated with criminals. A lot of people indirectly involved in big cases act like that. We usually hear them out and take no notice. But it was different with Bourguet. From what I could gather, he had friends high up in the police force. And he was a friend of the boss, and the boss of the *Crépu* is quite someone. He runs a big news agency that has influence with a lot of other papers. So Bourguet's name didn't appear anywhere else either.'

'Apparently the doctor didn't have the same scruples,' I said. 'There wasn't a single article where his name *wasn't* mentioned.'

'He was young and hadn't been qualified long. He couldn't have cared less. The fact that his car had played a part in the hold-up must have helped him get in with the cops . . . Talking of doctors, how's your cold?'

'Progressing.'

'I can hear that from your voice.'

He recommended the same barbaric-sounding remedy as Faroux. He took advantage of my gratitude to bombard me with questions. I eluded some, parried others, and then hung up.

I'd barely put the receiver down when the bell rang again. This time Hélène picked it up.

'It's Reboul,' she said. I grabbed it out of her hand.

'Spit it out!' I shouted.

'The man's name is Emmanuel Chabrot,' said Reboul calmly. 'He's been running a scandal sheet called *Q.E.D.* since before the war. He lived on the ground floor of a building in the rue Monsigny. That's where his office was, too. He went out this morning and returned home at midday. He obviously didn't intend to stay long, because he left his car outside with the engine running. He was probably just picking something up. He came out again at about twenty-five past, clutching his stomach and looking terrible, according to the people who saw him. Not surprising, with all that lead in him! Apparently he fell into his car and drove off in the direction of the centre of town. The killer came out almost as soon as Chabrot had gone, and hared off so fast no one could catch him. As usual, every witness gave a different description of him. But I interviewed one of Chabrot's neighbours, and he told me he'd heard the shots, though they were very muffled. And before that, the sound of an argument. He thought he heard someone shout: "It was you who put him on to us," and then some insults.'

'He said the shots were "muffled", did he?'

'Yes. I suppose the gun had a silencer on it.'

'Maybe. Was Chabrot shot in the stomach?'

'Yes.'

'From above or below?'

'Above, as you'd expect. Are you pleased with me?'

'Very.'

'Shall I go on with my inquiries?'

'No. Come back here and start on one of the new cases.'

I hung up and said to Hélène: 'Our new clients are going to have a fine opinion of the agency if we keep them hanging around like this . . . Hasn't anyone answered the advert yet?'

'No.'

I picked up my hat and left.

The avenue du Parc-des-Princes was basking in the March sunshine. Julien Bourguet's house was an opulent-looking detached villa on two floors, the lower one raised above ground level. I stood and looked at it for a moment. There didn't seem to be much activity going on inside, but I decided to try my luck.

A well-trained manservant answered the door-bell and told me Monsieur wasn't in but that his secretary was available.

'It's personal,' I said and gave him my card. 'Please tell Monsieur Bourguet I'll call again tomorrow morning.'

When I turned round, out in the street again, I thought I saw a curtain move on the first floor. But I couldn't see who was there.

I strolled about for a while, but the biting wind wasn't doing my cold any good. I met someone I knew, and he too suggested the famous panacea. So I went home in plenty of time to give it a try. It couldn't do me any harm, and I'd had enough of not being able to smoke.

13 Lydia confesses

After inhaling a lot of nauseating fumes I made myself a stiff grog, threw a double ration of coal on the stove and went to bed. My downstairs neighbour's radio was playing a foxtrot, and when that had finished some chap started making a speech. So I gave up trying to sleep and picked up a book.

I spent about an hour with it open at the same page, thinking, cursing the fact that I couldn't smoke, and listening to the sounds coming in from the street.

It was a peaceful night, even for a part of town that was usually quiet. The silence was broken from time to time by a car rushing past, someone's heels clacking on the pavement, or the brief whistle of a train.

I was roused from my reverie by the telephone. I looked at my watch. Half-past ten.

'Hallo.'

'Monsieur Nestor Burma?'

'Yes. What do you want?'

'It's Lydia Verbois.' She didn't need to tell me – I'd recognized her voice. This was the last thing I'd been expecting. 'I want to talk to you.'

'Go ahead.'

'Not on the telephone. At your place.'

'At this hour?'

'Yes.'

'We've exchanged roles,' I laughed. 'Now you're chasing me. How did you get hold of my address?'

'You're in the telephone directory.'

'True. So you want to see me that badly?'

'Yes.'

'But you've been running away up to now.'

'May I come or not?'

'Yes. The outside door's closed, but there's a bell. I'll come down when you ring.'

She hung up.

I got dressed again, put a bottle and two tumblers on a tray, and waited. At eleven my downstairs neighbour switched his radio on again, and I began thinking the lovely Lydia had taken me for a ride. Five minutes later I suddenly felt scared. Perhaps something had happened to her. Then the outside bell rang, I went down, and there waiting in the misty street was Lydia Verbois, safe and sound.

As we came up the stairs she missed a step.

'Tired?' I said.

'You live at the back of beyond.'

'Take your coat off,' I said once we were inside, 'and pull that armchair nearer the stove. Like some rum?'

'Yes, please.'

'Where did you call from? All the cafés are closed.'

'From my girlfriend's place.'

'Is it far from here?'

'It took me forty minutes.'

'Do you know what time it is?'

'Yes.'

'Do you have an *Ausweis*?'

'No.'

'So you're my prisoner until five tomorrow morning. Aren't you scared?'

'I wanted to talk to you.'

'You're a stubborn little creature. When you don't want to talk it's like trying to get blood out of a stone, and when you do want to talk there's no stopping you.'

She took off her turban-style hat and shook her hair free. Strands of gold spread over the leather back of the chair.

'I can't go on like this,' she whispered. 'I had to speak to someone. I'm surrounded by danger.'

I went over and laid my hand gently on her shoulder.

'Go ahead.'

She took a sip of the rum as if to give herself courage.

'I don't know how you're mixed up in all this, Monsieur Burma,' she said. 'But I feel I can trust you. I'm in a difficult situation. I wasn't just taking a shortcut through the building on the boulevard Victor that night. I lied to you. I'd arranged to meet Barton, and I was coming out of his room.'

'Barton or Briancourt?'

'What difference does it make?'

'A great deal. If it was Barton it means you'd known him for a long time. If it was Briancourt it means you could only have met him recently.'

'It was Barton.'

'So you knew what kind of a man he was.'

'He was my brother-in-law. The photo you showed me this afternoon was of my sister.'

'And the man with her was Barton?'

'Yes.'

'Go on.'

'Jeanne didn't know anything about Barton when she got involved with him. It was a terrible shock when she found out he was a criminal. She managed to get a divorce soon after he was sent to prison, and began a new life. She married a decent man and had a child. Now she lives quietly in the country.'

'I see. So it wouldn't have been very pleasant for her to bump into Barton again.'

'No. But that's what the wretched fellow wanted. I don't know how long he'd been in Paris, or how he got out of prison. But he was looking for her. The other day he was waiting for me when I came out of *Irma et Denise*.'

'Which day was that?'

'Monday. The day before – the day before it happened.'

'At lunch-time, or in the evening?'

'At lunch-time. I only had some drawings to take in that day, and I do that in the mornings. He walked down to the end of the road with me, making the most appalling threats. He wanted me to give him Jeanne's address. Then he suddenly changed his tune and said he'd be generous and give me time to think it over. He said he had my address and wasn't afraid of creating a scandal. Then he told me to come to his house the following day at eleven, and I agreed.'

She paused, and as her hand tensed on her knee, raising her skirt a little, I could see beneath a silk stocking the remains of the bruise she'd got when the Sloper and his mate tied her up.

'How did he know you'd be free to come at that time?' I said.

Her face clouded for a second.

'I don't know. I don't suppose he cared. It was an order, really.'

'So what happened?'

'I arrived on time. I'd prepared a speech to try and persuade him to be reasonable.' She gave a mirthless laugh. 'I found his room easily enough because there was a piece of paper with his name on it pinned to the door. I knocked, but there was no answer. I found the whole idea of the meeting repulsive, but I had to go through with it. So I tried the door, and it was open. I turned the handle, and . . . ' She buried her head in her hands. ' . . . He was lying there, dead.'

'How long had he been dead?'

'Do you think I went and looked? I stood there paralysed for a moment. His dying was . . . well, it was—'

'Too good to be true,' I said.

'It meant that Jeanne was free. That she'd never have to worry again about what he might be plotting. Seeing him lying there filled me with a kind of joy.'

'That's why you wouldn't have been too upset if a bomb had blown both him and the house to smithereens.'

'That's right. Then the sirens went off and I suddenly remembered where I was. I was afraid someone might see me there, and that they'd find the body and identify me as his sister-in-law. I panicked and ran away, and that's when I bumped into you. So you see why I didn't even stop when the air-raid warning went off, and why I got rid of you in the Métro . . . *And* why I drugged you that evening.'

She clutched my hand and looked up at me with eyes full of regret.

'Forgive me,' she whispered. 'I didn't know you were a friend.'

'Who says that I am?'

She dropped my hand dejectedly.

'You're not making things any easier for me.'

'Why should I?'

'I know I lied to you. But it was for Jeanne's sake — don't you understand? So she wouldn't be reminded of her hateful past. Then I decided that wasn't the best way, because your investigation was stirring up a lot of filth and some of it was bound to stick to her. You may say you're not a friend, but I can tell you're not an enemy. So I decided the wisest thing would be to come and tell you everything. Perhaps it was madness and I should have waited until tomorrow, but I wanted to come now.'

She shivered, and impetuously seized my hand again. Her eyes were moist and she looked at me imploringly.

'You do believe me, don't you?'

'Which bits do you want me to believe?'

'All of it. Everything I've said.'

I kept hold of her hand, and with my free one pulled a chair over and sat down.

'That's the trouble,' I said. 'You haven't told me everything.'

She slumped down in the armchair, her skirt riding up. But she didn't care – she was gazing through the glass door of the stove at the glowing anthracite inside, a mixture of suffering and resignation on her face. Neither of us spoke. Piano music drifted up from the radio downstairs.

'You've told me some of the things you're afraid of,' I said. 'But not all of them. You haven't told me who you suspect the murderer is, for example.'

'I don't suspect anyone!' she said.

'Yes, you do. You're afraid it might be your sister.'

'But she lives in the unoccupied zone,' she said desperately. 'She never comes to Paris. I haven't seen her for months.'

I shrugged.

'Why did you come to see me, then?'

'Can't you understand? So that you wouldn't suspect an innocent woman who's suffered more than enough already for marrying a criminal. I hoped once you knew the truth you'd avoid creating a scandal and shattering Jeanne's life all over again. I hoped you were a gentleman. But you're acting like a high-court judge. Worse – like a private detective. The police showed more respect for her at the time of the trial.'

She'd got up and was leaning on the back of the chair, quite out of breath after her outburst. I got up, too, and grabbed her by the arm.

'What do you mean, they showed respect for her?'

'They believed she was innocent, so they kept her out of the investigation and the trial.'

'I'm not as good as a real copper, is that it? I haven't as much tact, as much sense of decency, is that it?'

'You're a heartless monster!'

Now it was my turn to hold forth. The rum may have had something to do with it.

'And you're just a poor little kid who found herself face to face with a corpse and didn't know what to do! You thought the whole world was going to want explanations, and so at the first person you saw you panicked. What's more, you were sure the only person who could possibly want Barton out of the way was your sister, so you've spent the last three days thrashing around not knowing whether to tell the truth or to lie, and doing a bit of both. And when you finally did decide to come clean you couldn't carry it through. You're cool enough to contemplate spending the night alone with a man in his flat, but not to tell the whole truth. So you resort to insults. You're just a feather-brain, a bundle of contradictions, that's all. Does the description ring any bells?'

She turned away and put her hand to her forehead.

'You're very cruel,' she said.

'Not as cruel as you think, and I'm going to prove it. The only reason you're so worked up is you can't bear the thought of your sister being guilty.'

I took her by the shoulders and forced her to look at me.

'If I told you it was an idiotic idea would that pretty face relax a little?'

She blinked once or twice, but didn't answer.

'Let's try and talk this through,' I said. 'When you got into Barton's room he was already dead, wasn't he?'

She held my gaze and didn't hesitate for a second.

'Yes.'

'Good. That's quite possible. The doctor estimated the time of death at somewhere between ten o'clock in the morning and one o'clock in the afternoon. The killer could have got away without being seen, as you did. No one saw you go up or come down, so why shouldn't he have done the same? In fact, you were in more danger of being spotted than he was because of people going to and from the shelters. But what you say torpedoes the official version of Barton being killed during the raid itself. That was based on the fact that no one heard the shots, and I believed it too until I thought of the possibility of a silencer. The police didn't think of it because as far as they're concerned silencers exist only in books. I've only recently come round to the idea that the murderer must have used one: there's always enough noise going on in an apartment block to cover the sound of a pistol with a silencer, air raid or no air raid. And if one was used it means the killer had a certain kind of mentality. I don't think your sister is the kind of person to do a thing like that. But men like the two who attacked you out at Bois-le-Roi the other night might have.'

'You think it was them who—'

'They must fit into the story somewhere,' I said.

'What did they want from me then?' she faltered. The mere thought of what had happened made her scared all over again.

'If I knew we wouldn't be sitting here drinking my cellar

dry,' I said, pouring myself another glass. 'Barton's jacket was hanging over the back of a chair. You didn't notice anything unusual about it, did you?'

'No. I was too upset.'

'Are you sure?'

'I swear. Why, what was so special about it?'

'Nothing. And the table?'

'The table?'

'Yes. Didn't you notice anything on the table?'

'No, nothing at all. I couldn't take my eyes off—'

'There were ten thousand francs in notes of fifty and a hundred francs on the table. I haven't seen them myself, but that's what the cops told me. It wasn't you who left them there, was it?'

'No. Why should I have gone there with money?'

She sat down in the armchair again.

'To persuade Barton to leave your sister in peace . . . Look,' I said, leaning forward encouragingly. 'It doesn't make any difference whether you left the money or not now. It's just a question of straightening out what really happened. You went in carrying the money, hoping to spend as little time with the fellow as possible. When you saw what had happened you were so upset you automatically put the money down on the table and forgot to pick it up again when you ran away. Isn't that what happened?'

'No,' she said firmly.

'Really?'

'I'd never go to see a man like that carrying all that money.'

I studied her face intently, then patted her on the shoulder.

'Good,' I said. 'I was virtually sure someone else had done it. But if you'd gone along with my explanation—'

'You mean it was a trap?'

'Are you angry?'

She smiled sadly.

'You're very funny,' she said.

'And your perfume is delightful.' (This was no doubt true, but thanks to my cold I could only draw a bow at a venture.) 'What is it?'

'Is this another trap?'

'Oh, that's unkind . . . You don't have to answer.'

'I know that. It's called *Valence*. It's lavender scent, by Charon, in case you were thinking of buying me a bottle.'

'Why not?' I said, smiling.

Downstairs the sound of the radio had been replaced by the snoring of its owner. I went to get another half-bottle of rum from the cupboard.

The silence of the night was broken by the striking of a distant clock. A gentle warmth pervaded the room. Neither of us knew what to talk about.

'If you want to rest until the Métro opens . . . ' I said.

'No, thank you. I'm quite comfortable by the fire.'

I refilled our glasses and we chatted about this and that, avoiding the subject that was uppermost in our thoughts. But I couldn't help turning it over in my mind. And I could tell by Lydia's silence that she was doing the same.

'What are you thinking about?' I said at one point.

'Nothing,' she said. 'And you?'

'What do you *think* I'm thinking about?' I was preoccupied with Barton, the midget, *Q.E.D.* and a host of similar problems.

She stretched like a cat. Her arms and legs quivered, and her bosom stood out tautly against her silk blouse. She looked at me provocatively.

'What *does* a man think about when he's alone with a woman?'

'Look here . . . ' I stammered.

I stood up. My head was throbbing and felt like lead, partly because of the rum and partly because my cold had reached the stage where I had to keep my mouth open to breathe. I looked more like an expiring goldfish than a suave seducer.

'Lydia,' I said, and took a step towards the chair where she lay back invitingly.

I was dragged from sleep by a strident ringing. I felt for the alarm clock and turned it off, but the ringing continued. It was the telephone. I switched on the bedside light, and Lydia turned over to escape the glare and the noise. Nearly four o'clock. I picked up the phone.

'Monsieur Nestor Burma?'

A woman's voice.

'Yes.'

'Madame Julien Bourguet here. I thought I'd be sure to get you at this hour. You arranged to come and see my husband later this morning, I believe.' Her voice was tense and abrupt, and she was speaking quietly but precisely, with her mouth against the receiver so she wouldn't have to repeat anything. Her spouse was obviously asleep nearby.

'That's correct,' I said.

'I must see you first. May I come to your office at half-past nine?'

'Yes.'

She hung up without another word.

I hung up with a crash, completely baffled.

14 The woman in the taxi

The 'flu' treatment that Faroux, Covet and Co. had recommended really was effective, as I realized when the Métro broke down and I was trapped inside with all the time in the world to savour the smell. I was also late for my appointment.

When Hélène saw me she burst out laughing and offered me a handkerchief.

'You've been in action early,' she said. 'You'd better wipe your mouth or we'll have a crime of passion on our hands: there's *another woman* waiting next door. She's been here for twenty minutes.'

She also told me a man named Friant had turned up in answer to the advertisement, but he was so unprepossessing she hadn't wanted to take the responsibility of hiring him. He was coming back later.

I removed the traces of Lydia's last kiss and went through into my office.

Madame Julien Bourguet was sitting on a chair by the wall, clutching a copy of the *Journal de Paris* in her gloved hands. She was about thirty, and elegantly if rather austerely dressed, with a pretty face completely devoid of make-up. She'd have been very attractive were it not for the bitter twist to her mouth and the nervous tic that made her keep tossing her head. Everything about her exuded suffering.

I apologized for being late and suggested she might find an armchair more comfortable. She perched on the edge of one as if about to take flight at any moment. My cold was fading, so I asked politely whether she'd mind if I smoked.

'If you like,' she said carelessly. 'I'm surprised you're so genteel as to ask. But I didn't come here to discuss etiquette . . . Why are you so interested in that bastard Barton's death?'

I was surprised that she was so vulgar.

'What makes you think I *am* interested?' I said.

'Never you mind – I know. That's not what I came here to talk about.'

'What did you come here to talk about?'

'You know very well,' she snapped, her twitch becoming even more pronounced. 'So why don't we—'

I couldn't resist interrupting, to show how brilliant I was.

'Is that the paper you usually read?' I asked.

'Yes.'

'I know it's not what you came here to talk about, but you saw my advertisement in yesterday's edition, printed by accident right in the middle of the piece about Barton. I've got an unusual name – it stuck in your mind. And yesterday evening you saw it again: no doubt, after peering out at me from behind the curtains as I lurked round your house, you asked the butler who the strange visitor was and he showed you my card. You put two and two together: Barton, the Thévenon case, Dynamite Burma and your husband – and you decided to not to tell Monsieur Bourguet anything about my having called. That's what happened, isn't it?'

'Yes,' she said, clearly taken aback.

'So what *was* the connection?'

She fiddled with her gloves and compressed her lips.

'You know very well.'

She was right. Certain things were beginning to dawn on me.

I leaned forward.

'I wanted to ask your husband why he was so keen to keep his name out of the papers at the time of the Thévenon affair. Perhaps you can tell me instead?'

She sprang to her feet.

A wad of hundred- and fifty-franc notes fell on to my desk.

'Will that be enough?' she said.

'I didn't know you ran a charity,' I said.

She didn't answer.

'Relax,' I said. 'Why did you call Barton a bastard?'

Hatred flashed in her eyes, her mouth worked silently, her tic became more violent. Then she turned deathly white and crashed to the floor.

I called out for Hélène. She came running in, then stopped and gave a whistle.

'You certainly do slay them,' she said.

'This is no time for joking,' I said. 'Help me bring her round. But first, what perfume's this?'

I waved a bank-note under her nose.

She sniffed.

'"Last Night",' she said.

I whipped a handkerchief out of my pocket.

'And this? Is it the same?'

'No. That's—'

'Some other time,' I said.

While Hélène set about reviving our visitor, I went through her handbag. But there was nothing unusual about it, except that it was saturated with the famous perfume. I also retrieved my visiting card.

Madame Bourguet was coming round, her lips moving feebly. I bent over her, but couldn't make out a word. Then Hélène came to the rescue.

'Just now she murmured "Fred", or something like that,' she said.

'Alfred,' I said. 'Thévenon's Christian name. She was his mistress.'

Hélène was so surprised she let go of the woman's head, which fell back on to the floor.

'Don't kill her, for God's sake!' I said.

It had quite the opposite result. Madame Bourget tried to sit up, and looked around her in a daze. When we got her into an armchair she hid her face in her hands.

'Please!' she sobbed. 'Don't torture me any more.'

But I realized that if I pushed her a bit she'd give me some interesting information.

'You were Thévenon's mistress,' I said evenly. 'You were the mysterious woman in the taxi. Your husband realized it must be you, but he's a decent chap and instead of throwing you out he tried to save you. So now you want to spare him any painful reminders of the past, and that's why you're here. That's it, isn't it?'

'You know very well it is.'

'There are some things I don't know, though. For example whether, during your taxi ride, Thévenon told you where he'd hidden the gold.'

'Is it the gold you're interested in?'

'Among other things. I'm also interested in Barton's murder.'

'He got what was coming to him!' she hissed.

'He was no great loss, I admit. But why did he deserve to die?'

'It was because of him that Alfred was executed.'

'I know you loved him,' I said, 'but he was a criminal, a crook, a cad – he deliberately involved you in the hold-up by using your car . . . Even so, you were mad enough to go with him in the taxi.'

'I always loved him,' she said. Her voice had gone dull and expressionless. 'I was cold to him only once, and that's when everything started going wrong. It broke his heart. He went off and started planning the hold-up – it was his way of committing suicide. I knew from the start that he'd got on the wrong side of the law – he told me so. But he'd never killed anyone before. He was a swindler, that's all. When I found out he carried a gun I took it away – that was silly though, because it's quite easy to replace them . . . *He* didn't steal our car – it was one of the other members of the gang, who didn't even know me. It was just a terrible coincidence, but Alfred killed him for it just the same . . . He told me so in the taxi. He told me everything in the taxi . . . As soon as I read the papers after the hold-up, I recognized our car from the description and knew Alfred had something to do with it. But I'm the guilty one, for that one moment of misunderstanding . . . Forgive me, Julien – it's Alfred I love. Alfred, our guest, our friend. And he's the man they're after. But he needn't be linked to us if we don't say anything.'

Then, still in the same tone, she seemed to be assuming the character of Julien.

'Yes. You're right. There's no reason why I should give evidence without being asked. We must do everything possible to keep our name out of it.'

She paused, still in another world. One of the few cars still on the road in war-time Paris went past, hooting at the crossroads.

'The taxi,' she said. 'I agreed to come because I was

sorry for you. But now I know how much I love you. I'll always love you, no matter what. Let's run away, the two of us! What? – it's all over? Give yourself up? That would put an end to it all? The end? The end of you! Oh, but I love you, I always will!'

For a moment I thought she was going to faint again. Her pallor increased, her eyes stared wildly. Then she seemed to come out of her trance, and her voice returned to normal.

'Haven't I suffered enough?'

She let Hélène pat her hand, but her eyes were fixed on mine.

'All right,' I said. 'As soon as you feel better you can go home. I won't go and see your husband. I've got all I wanted.'

She didn't say a word. She just gave a sigh and seemed to plunge deep in thought. But the awful tic, the involuntary tossing of the head, left her no respite.

'You've been like that ever since the joyride, eh?'

She closed her eyes, meaning this was so. Then suddenly started up like an automaton and prepared to leave, still without speaking. I gathered together the banknotes scattered over the desk.

'Have you often been blackmailed?' I said.

She gave a horrible little laugh:

'Afraid you're only the last in a long line of sharks?'

'Paying in notes this small makes it look as if you might have done it before.'

'I read about it somewhere.'

'Do you read a lot?'

'Yes.'

'American books too?'

'Yes.'

'Do you know about the Chicago dollar?'

'No.'

She'd had enough. It wasn't surprising. I put the notes into her hand.

'Goodbye,' I said. 'I'm not *Q.E.D.*, you know.'

'But you said you'd got all you wanted—'

'I wasn't referring to the money.'

Again she went pale with terror.

'Would . . . would twenty thousand be enough?' she stammered.

I pushed her gently towards the door.

'Nothing at all,' I said. 'Go home now. Perhaps I'll telephone you one of these days.'

She still wasn't very steady on her feet as she went out through the door.

'That's what you get for falling in love,' I said to Hélène. 'Be warned!'

She shrugged in annoyance.

'Poor woman,' she said.

'Never mind about that. Tell me what you know about "Last Night",' I said.

She was vexed at my cynicism.

'It wasn't popular at first,' she said curtly. 'Now nine women out of ten use it. And with all the money they spend on publicity, the others will soon follow suit.'

'You seem to know a lot about it.'

'I was one of the few who wore it before the war. I gave it up when my cleaning lady started using it.'

'No need to be sniffy about cleaning ladies! I could do with one around here – I can't find my bull's-head pipe in all this mess!'

That did it.

'What you really need is a detective!' she said.

15 The agency takes on staff

It was a little after eleven. I'd just been examining some auburn hairs that had been in my possession since the night before, and had decided their marvellous colour was natural, when Pierre Friant, the candidate for the new job, turned up.

He was middle-aged, unattractive and ill-shaven, with shifty eyes in an indiarubber face framed between a pair of protruding ears. He looked worn out, and so did his clothes. He breathed in the smoke from my pipe with a mixture of delight and longing, then introduced himself in a flat monotone, twisting his cap between his fingers.

I asked him for his references.

'I hope you won't want me to do anything too tricky,' he said, 'I've never worked in this line before. It may sound funny coming from a man of forty, but I don't mind how small the job is. I need the work.'

I could well believe it. But I was also sure what he'd said about never having done detective work before was a lie.

'I need someone urgently,' I said, 'so I'll take you on trial. Go and see my secretary. She'll give you something to do that you could manage with your eyes shut. But before you start, tell her you want a brush for your trousers, another for your shoes, and something respectable to replace that cap. And unless you made a New Year's resolution to stop shaving, go to the barber's and get the beard removed.'

When he'd gone off to ruin at least one client's impression of the Fiat Lux Agency, I asked Hélène to ring round all our competitors and ask them if a man named Pierre Friant had ever worked for them.

The first two replies were negative. As soon as the third person picked up the phone and realized who was calling, he started kicking up a fuss about a case that had caused some friction between us five years before. Hélène went bright red and hung up. His language must have been even worse than mine. Then she called a fourth number and turned up trumps. Lucien Arribore *had* employed Friant. He said he wasn't a bad detective, but had an unfortunate habit of trying to make money for himself instead of for his employer. Arribore had given him the sack a year ago.

'So do *we* keep him?' asked Hélène, who was obviously in favour of giving him the Arribore treatment.

'For the moment. We can always let him go if a better candidate comes along.'

It was lunch-time by now, and I went and joined Lydia in an intimate restaurant where Cupid's bow had been replaced by a machine-gun. On the way I bought a copy of *Paris-Midi*: it had a paragraph on the Barton case. The investigation continued. The police now suspected a woman of committing the murder, but the paper didn't say why.

We said goodbye under a poster advertising the Médrano circus. There was no mention of Mac's name among the performers, so I went into the nearest café to call his hotel and try to get some news. They told me he'd gone away. I hung up and called one of Faroux's favourite stamping grounds, a restaurant in the Place Dauphine. He was there.

'What's this?' I said. 'Swapping suspects every day now, are we? How did you come to the conclusion it was a woman?'

'The perfume.'

He didn't sound all that pleased.

'I thought it was the perfume that got Lofty into trouble.'

'He's been crossed off the list,' he said, sounding more and more lugubrious. 'His confession didn't ring true to one of my colleagues' – clearly someone Faroux couldn't stand – 'and he found out what Mac was really doing during the air raid. He was down in the hotel cellar with his teeth chattering. There's no doubt about it.'

He seemed really disappointed.

'Does he scare easily?'

'In air raids, yes.'

'Well, I've got a tip for you. He's hopped it.'

'How do you know?'

'I've just rung his hotel.'

'What for? Ah, of course, you wanted to see him. What about?'

'Nothing.'

He gave a bitter laugh.

'You can't be in that much of a hurry, then! Anyway, don't worry about him. We're keeping him inside for a bit, just to teach him a lesson.'

He hung up and I went back to the agency in a bad temper. I was still feeling tetchy when Hélène said Pierre Friant was back.

After a shave and brush-up he looked in better shape, and he gave a concise account of his handling of the case he'd been assigned to. Once or twice he made as if to take something out of his pocket, and I noticed the tips of his fingers were stained. When he'd finished I called Hélène.

'Have you given Monsieur Friant an advance?' I said.

'No.'

I got up. Friant saw what was coming. I grabbed him by the collar, yanked him to his feet, and brought his face close to mine. His breath reeked of tobacco. I felt in his pocket and brought out a packet of Gauloises that had already been started and another with nothing but butt-ends in it.

I threw the whole lot on the desk.

'You're like me in one thing at least,' I said. 'You go crazy without tobacco. I noticed it this morning by the way you sniffed my pipe smoke. You were broke then, and tobacco's expensive. You shouldn't be any richer now, but you've got two hundred and fifty francs-worth of cigarettes there. A hundred and twenty-five, rather: I can tell by your fingers you've smoked half of them already – they weren't that yellow this morning. Where did you get the money from?'

He started to say something like 'Mind your own damn business,' but I didn't wait to hear it all – I wasn't in the mood. My fist caught him on the chin, and he went sprawling on to the floor. Hélène looked on smiling.

Before he could get up I was on top of him.

'You're crooked, Monsieur Pierre Friant,' I said. 'Lucien Arribore told me so, and for once he was right. You've made a deal with our client behind my back, haven't you? Or perhaps he was under the impression you were going to give the money to me. Which is it?'

He mumbled something indistinct, but clear enough to be recognized as offensive.

'I'm ready to go on with this for some time,' I said. 'I may not feel too good myself, but I can certainly outclass you.'

He tried to say something else, and I realized he couldn't because my knee was on his chest. I took it away and he climbed to his feet. Then, eyeing the cigarettes on my desk all the time, he told us what had happened at M. Guy Duval's, in the rue Cardinet.

'When I got there he asked me if I was new here, and I said yes, I'd only been taken on about an hour ago. He said that didn't matter, and we started chatting about the case – so-called, because in the end he admitted it was all a hoax. A kind of joke, he said. He hadn't got time to carry it out himself, but if I did it for him I wouldn't regret it. So I was all ears, and we made a deal. He wanted me to keep you in the dark, but carry on as if I was genuinely doing an investigation for a few days, and then make it look as if I'd reached a dead end. I agreed, and he paid me . . . er . . . a thousand francs.'

'Two thousand,' I said. 'Try to get out of the habit of lying.'

'All right – two thousand.'

'Tell me what he looks like. Is he young, with a sloping forehead, a long nose, swivel eyes and a slick moustache?'

'That's it. Except for the moustache.'

'He's shaved it off. What sort of place does he live in?'

'I don't think it's where he lives. More like a pied-à-terre.'

'It's no good going to see if he's still at home, then,' I said to Hélène. 'The Sloper will have sloped off by now.'

I thought for a moment, then pushed the cigarettes across the desk towards our new recruit. He lit up at once, then said uncomfortably:

'I suppose you'll be—'

'No, I won't,' I said. 'You can stay on. But you'll be working for me, is that clear? You'll carry on as though none of this had happened and do what Duval tells you. Concoct reports and all the rest of it. But you'll have to make it look good. As if you really wanted to string me along. And keep your mouth shut . . . We'll see later on whether we can give you another assignment.'

'I get it,' he said.

He was eating out of my hand.

On the stroke of three Hélène brought in another visitor: a pleasant, nicely turned out young man with a pair of bright eyes behind his glasses. Hélène was obviously impressed. He too had come about the job. At first I thought he must have come to the wrong place, and told him Grimault's, the film company, were on the floor below. He smiled, introduced himself as Laurent Gaillard, and said in cultivated but slightly lilting accents that he'd broken with the tradition of detectives being got up any old how when he'd worked for Auguste.

'Auguste in Lyons?' I said.

'Yes. I had that honour,' he said, holding out his references. I ran an eye over them and then gave them back.

'I don't know,' I said. 'A good detective has to blend into the landscape and be in good physical condition. Your glasses are a problem.'

He laughed gaily.

'They're plain glass,' he said, showing them to me. 'It's just camouflage. I can see perfectly well without them.'

'Excellent!' I said, shaking him by the hand. 'Welcome to the Fiat Lux Agency! Let me introduce my secretary, Hélène.'

'We've already met,' he said rather smugly.

'Good Lord!' I said. 'You're quick off the mark. We'll get on well.'

Hélène gave him his instructions in a languishing voice and he went off. I'd put my coat on and was about to leave myself when the phone rang. Hélène answered. It was

Reboul, asking for some information. When he'd got it from her I took the phone.

'How's it going?' I said.

'All right.'

'Nothing out of the ordinary?'

'No.'

'Good. Shelve it for the moment. Find me the witness who heard the shots when Chabrot copped it, and get him to come to the agency tomorrow morning – no, the café opposite would be better. I'll have him brought up from there. Got it?'

'Got it.'

I hung up.

'Have you found my bull's-head pipe yet, Hélène?' I said.

'I haven't looked for it.'

'Never mind – smoking's not allowed in the library anyway.'

'What are you going *there* for again?'

'To go over all the material on the train robbery. There are lots of things I still don't understand.'

16 Suicide

That very same evening my wretched pipe was the cause of our first row.

I'd been hunting for it a good hour, scattering the others I kept in my chest of drawers right and left, some of them in pieces, and sending a Ropp that was getting on my nerves flying around the room. Lydia remarked that if I was often in this kind of mood, life together looked promising. Then, swathing herself in the elegant dressing gown she'd collected from her friend's place when we decided she might as well move in with me, she sighed, shrugged, opened a book the wrong way up and went into a sulk.

I solemnly swore I'd find the prize item in my collection if it took me until the next world war, and went on with my search. A quarter of an hour later the chaos was at its height, and I was inventing new and elaborate swear-words.

Finally I flung open the wardrobe so roughly that a box perched precariously on a shelf came crashing down in a cloud of dust, choking and blinding me and eliciting my most original blasphemy yet.

Then I saw my jacket still damp from the day before, and it occurred to me that I must have left the pipe I was looking for in one of the pockets.

I was right. I was just about to dust off my treasure, when . . .

I was speechless. I couldn't even swear. I looked at the clock. Eleven. I rushed to the phone. The *Crépu* had been bringing out a morning edition for some time now, so Marc must be there. Faroux would have been better, but I didn't fancy letting him into my secret.

The whole world seemed to be against me. Now the telephone was on the blink. I managed to get through at the fifth attempt. Marc too seemed very het up. His 'Hallo?' almost split my eardrums.

'I've been trying to get hold of you for ages!' he yelped.

'What about *me*?' I said. 'I've been ringing for the last ten minutes! Anyway, what did you want to say?'

'I know you're interested in Julien Bourguet. Well, his wife committed suicide this afternoon.'

'What!'

'And she used a rather unusual weapon for a respectable member of the bourgeoisie: a 7.65 revolver fitted with a silencer.'

'What!'

'You heard!'

'Stay where you are. I'm coming over. It'll take me an hour and a half, and it's a cold night for a walk – but what I've got to tell you is well worth it.'

I hung up, took my bull's-head carefully by the end of the stem, put it in a box so that its horns touched the sides and held it firmly in place, then flung my coat on, put the box in my pocket and grabbed my hat.

'I have to go out,' I said.

'Glad to get away from me, I suppose?'

'No. Just glad to find I've been barking up the wrong tree.'

*

It was after midnight by the time I got there. The *Crépu* building was a sinister place at that hour. My footsteps echoed down its cold empty corridors as the muffled thud of the presses drifted up from the basement. The whole place was plunged in darkness. Or almost. A single ray of light filtered under the door of Marc Covet's office.

He was waiting for me, a well-broached bottle of wine beside him on the desk. While I finished it off he filled me in on the details of his sensational discovery.

The news of Madame Bourguet's suicide had been announced by a press agency, along with that of four or five other people. But given the shortage of newsprint, that sort of thing was destined for the waste-paper basket. However, Marc spotted it, and set off at once to do a bit of investigating on his own account in the avenue du Parc-des-Princes. That's how he'd found out that Madame Bourguet had used a pistol with a silencer. By now he was really intrigued, and was sure I knew more about it than he did.

'Just sit back and relax,' I said. 'I've got a real surprise for you. Madame Bourguet was Thévenon's mistress. The woman in the taxi.'

Marc's jaw dropped.

I went on to recount her visit to my office the previous morning, and how she'd attempted to buy my silence.

'She seemed quite familiar with the system,' I said. 'She must have lived in a permanent fear of being blackmailed. The money they found at Barton's place came out of her handbag. She'd gone there to pay him off, but her feelings for Thévenon must have revived, and when she found herself face to face with the man who'd betrayed him she lost her head, pulled out the gun and shot him.'

'But what about the silencer?' said Marc. 'That suggests the murder was premeditated.'

'Not necessarily. The gun was no doubt the one she'd

taken away from Thévenon and kept ever since. The silencer had been on it for ages, and it never occurred to her to take it off. Not even before she killed herself. People don't usually bother about keeping their own suicide quiet.'

'But she *did* go to Barton's with a gun.'

'Just a precaution. Blackmailers can be dangerous.'

Marc shook his head and squinted at the tip of his nose. He wasn't convinced.

'You go to see a blackmailer either to pay him off or to do him in. Not both.'

'But a woman in her state of mind doesn't act logically. Anyway, Barton wasn't killed deliberately.'

'Oh, you were there, were you?'

'Madame Bourguet was of average height. How do you think she shot him in the stomach from below? By kneeling down?'

'You've got a point there. So?'

'So Barton didn't intend to blackmail her, as she'd imagined – he just wanted some information from her. It must have happened something like this: she goes in and puts the money down, and Barton comes towards her, saying quietly, so as to avoid letting the whole building know about it, that there'd been a misunderstanding. But she thinks his manner is threatening, draws back, trips and falls to her knees. Then a whole lot of things rush through her mind: the need to defend herself, memories of Thévenon, and the fact that here is the chance to avenge his death. She pulls out her revolver and fires . . . That would explain the distance and the angle of the shot.'

'Then what *did* Barton want, if he wasn't interested in the money?'

'The gold.'

'Good God!'

'It's about time you gave it a thought too,' I said. 'I've

just been going through the press accounts of the hold-up again. There was no mention of the missing ingots until Thévenon gave himself up to the police. Barton was already inside by then. Had been since the 8th. So he must have found out about it from his lawyer, and imagined, like everyone else, that the only person in on Thévenon's secret was the woman in the taxi. I'm convinced Barton himself *didn't* know where the gold was, even if Hélène and several other people think he did, and that he denounced Thévenon to keep it for himself. After Barton was repatriated from Germany and released with the other POWs in the unoccupied zone, he rushed back to Paris as soon as he could, though he'd have been safer staying on in the south. He didn't even wait for the special train that runs up to Paris about every two months. I suppose he must have known for some time who the woman in the taxi was. So once he got back he began to track her down. As well as another person he was after for quite different reasons.

'But he was very careful. He didn't go back to his flat until he'd found out there was a new concierge, and even then only after dark. If he'd gone on like that he wouldn't have found them for months, but last Monday was his lucky day – much luckier than Tuesday! By an enormous fluke, just as he was getting discouraged and had decided to get me to help him, he found both the people he was looking for at practically the same time.'

'What!' said Marc.

'Yes! You didn't know that, did you?'

Then I told him as much as I thought he needed to know.

'Terrific!' he said, his nose twitching and going redder than ever. 'What a marvellous article it would make!'

'"Would make"? You're still a journalist, aren't you?' I said.

'You don't think they'd publish anything about that now, do you? The file I've built up is just for my own satisfaction. But I'll add all this to it. So keep going, and tell me why a woman tough enough to go through with the taxi episode and to commit a murder should suddenly have thrown in the towel.'

'Her nerves finally cracked,' I said. 'She never really got over the taxi-ride – I could see that yesterday morning. She killed Barton instinctively, not deliberately. And the way she tried to keep me quiet was painfully clumsy. Someone as neurotic as that could only have felt worse after seeing the way I reacted, so when she read in the paper that the police suspected a woman of the murder, she just gave up the struggle and killed herself.'

'That figures,' said Marc.

'It certainly does. Barton was killed by a 7.65 mm, and nobody heard. Madame Bourget committed suicide with a gun of the same calibre fitted with a silencer. Have the police put two and two together yet?'

'I don't know.'

'They must have. Still, it won't do any harm to let them know they're not the only ones with bright ideas. Keep them in their place!'

I picked up a note that was lying around from a reader of the *Crépu* who didn't know there was a war on – most of the sheet was left blank – and typed a little anonymous letter. Then I addressed a cheap brown envelope to Inspector Florimond Faroux at 36 quai des Orfèvres, wiped paper and envelope off with my handkerchief, put on my gloves, slipped the letter inside, unsigned, and sealed it. Marc found these precautions hilarious, but I told him you needed to be careful even if the police didn't have your fingerprints. The bloke who'd sent them Thévenon's pistol in 1938 was going to be sorry he hadn't been equally prudent.

Marc shot me a meaning look.

'It sounds as if you'd got more revelations up your sleeve,' he said.

'Yes. But I'll tell you only on condition you keep on good terms with your informant at the CID. I need a photograph of the famous fingerprint with the cross on it. I want to check up on something.'

'The person in question's dead,' said Marc. 'But that's neither here nor there. What about my own file? It's just as complete as the one the cops have got, and it's got a facsimile of the print you're talking about.'

I took the box out of my pocket, extracted the pipe and held it so that the light fell full on it. There on the polished bowl, highlighted by the dust, was a thumbprint with two narrow scars in the form of a cross.

'Holy smoke!' growled Marc. 'I'd recognize that anywhere.'

I left Marc Covet's flat at four in the morning, convinced that the print on my pipe and the one found on Thévenon's revolver had been made by the same thumb.

On my way home I marked the little brown envelope 'Urgent' and put it into the box for *pneumatiques** near the Cité Métro.

When I got home Lydia was asleep, her beautiful innocent face buried in the pillow. It was such a peaceful scene there were a lot of things I began to regret.

I called Reboul and woke him up. Knowing who'd killed

---

* *Translator's note*: the *pneumatique* system – a cheap and efficient form of telegram – carried notes and letters in air-driven metal cylinders by an underground system of tubes to any destination in Paris and the suburbs from 1859 until it was discontinued, much to the chagrin of lovers, in 1984.

Barton and who'd sent the revolver to the police didn't mean I could neglect the *Q.E.D.* gang.

Reboul told me sleepily that he hadn't been able to find the witness he was looking for. I told him to forget about the meeting we'd arranged for next morning. I had other fish to fry.

17 A pillar of society

Marc Covet arrived at nine o'clock. His eyelids were swollen and almost as red as his nose. Unlike me he hadn't slept well.

When he saw Lydia he winked and said he hoped all our troubles would be little ones. I said I'd be careful, in case there was any chance of their turning out like him.

After this witty exchange we went down to the car Marc had managed to get hold of. We didn't say much during the drive. The weather was overcast, and coming out of the forest of Sénart there was a real downpour. But by the time we got to Bois-le-Roi the weather had improved.

I managed to find the rue Albert-Blain again without too much trouble, and at Jander's place the same woman as before – the one I guessed was his wife – answered the door. As soon as I opened my mouth she said she was sorry but Monsieur Jander had only just got up. Perhaps we'd like to come back later . . .

'Not a chance,' I said. 'We want to see him now . . . Come on, Marc.'

I pushed past her and we went inside just as a door opened and the owner of the house appeared. He was wearing a moth-eaten dressing gown and a skullcap, and his angry face was neither washed nor shaven. But he already had a pipe in his mouth.

'What do you mean by—' he began.

'I've come to give you bit of advice,' I said, pushing him back through the door he'd just come out of. 'Be careful when you handle other people's property.'

'I don't know what you're talking about, and if you don't clear off I'll call the police.'

I got to the telephone before he did and put my hand over the receiver.

'Don't be a fool, Jander,' I said. 'Ask your wife to leave us alone. We need to talk.'

He took no notice, so I let him have the phone. But as he leaned forward to take it I whispered something in his ear.

He dropped the receiver, his pipe fell from his mouth, and he went as white as a sheet.

'How? . . . How on earth . . . ?' he stammered.

'Pull yourself together,' I said. 'We're not going to eat you.'

He tried to smile, but managed only a sort of grimace.

'Leave me to deal with this,' he said to his wife, who was clearly taken aback. 'They're just a couple of practical jokers.'

He shut the door behind her, drew a heavy curtain over it, then turned back towards us. He looked suddenly older: fear was written all over his usually self-satisfied face.

'How did you guess?' he managed to gasp at last.

'That doesn't matter – I know, that's all. You're the one who's got to do the explaining. I want the whole story.'

He still hesitated.

'I told you I was a private detective,' I said. 'But there could be more to it than that. And my friend here passes for an ordinary journalist. But look at the evidence he's got.'

I showed him the photograph of the thumbprint.

'You left that mark on Thévenon's revolver. The finger-print boys have been comparing it with every new set of dabs for the last four years: they'd give a lot to be in my shoes now. So I'll tell you straight out – if you won't talk to me you'll find yourself talking to the CID . . . Whereas if you *do* come clean now—'

'How do I know I can trust you?' he mumbled.

'I'm Nestor Burma,' I said. 'A private detective. I don't work for society – society's big enough to look after itself – I work for myself and my own interests. But when I fight, I fight.'

'That's a very selfish point of view,' he began. He looked quite disapproving. Even with the wind up he was still a stick-in-the-mud. Marc and I hooted with laughter.

'We'll come back another time for the lecture on morals,' I said. 'With a teacher like you it'll be quite something. Now let's get back to the present!'

'I suppose I might as well tell you everything,' he said. 'You probably know it all already.'

'Tell me anyway.'

'And you might as well sit down, too,' said Covet, who'd already made himself at home.

Jander obeyed, twiddling his pipe between his fingers and casting rueful glances every now and then at the tell-tale scars on his thumb.

'No one ever found out where Thévenon holed up after the train robbery in '38,' he began. 'Well, gentlemen, it was in my house. Not this one! A little villa I own in l'Allée du Platane—'

I couldn't help starting.

Jander noticed and paused, but I told him to go on.

'It's not an easy place to let, and at the end of 1937 I was pleased to be able to lease it to a very pleasant young man called Albert Tannier. Though he did wear a bohemian sort of beard he was quiet and well behaved, and he lived in the house on and off until the middle of January '38. Then, apart from one or two short absences, he stayed there for about a month. And suddenly, on 22 February, he disappeared. I don't remember why or how, but a week or so later it suddenly struck me there might be a connection between his vanishing and the arrest of the famous gangster all the papers were talking about. The fact that he hardly ever went away during the period immediately after the hold-up began to worry me. So I looked at the newspaper photographs of Thévenon carefully, and with one or two modifications it was clearly the same man. I decided there was no point in telling the police. The house was so isolated it was difficult enough to let already – if a criminal was known to have lived there I'd never get it off my hands again. So I made up my mind to say nothing. After all, Thévenon had been caught, and that was the main thing.'

'Quite,' I said. 'And keeping quiet left your hands free.'

'To find a new tenant, yes.'

'To look for the gold, you mean! The papers were talking of nothing else, and rumour had it that wherever Thévenon had been hiding for the last three weeks, that's where the gold was too. So you thought: why not look for it yourself?'

Jander gulped. It took him a moment to get over his surprise. Then he unscrewed the stem of his pipe, which seemed to inject a bit of energy into him, and gave me the clear-eyed stare of someone who pays his taxes regularly but doesn't hesitate to travel first class with a second-class ticket.

'Exactly,' he said almost defiantly. 'I began searching immediately, and carried on looking till 1941. Then I decided to let the house again. It wasn't bringing in a centime, and I hadn't found anything at all.'

'What about the revolver?'

'That was the only reward for all my efforts.'

'Where did you find it?'

'I thought for a moment I'd found the swag.'

'What do you mean?'

'I'd concentrated on the cellar, because Tannier had mixed some cement down there one day. At the time I pretended not to notice, because I thought he must be doing some repairs and I didn't want to foot the bill. But hearing about the gold changed everything. I thought he'd probably built a kind of safe for it in the wall. And I was right – except that the gold bars weren't there. I found the safe quite easily, but what was inside it? Just the gun. Incriminating evidence – not surprising that he wanted to get rid of it.'

'And cementing it into a wall was safer than chucking it into the river,' I murmured.

'The revolver!' Jander went on loudly, like a lawyer interrupted by a feeble joke, 'gave me irrefutable proof of Thévenon's guilt. And it was my duty, as a respectable citizen, to advance the cause of justice.'

'Especially as it would have been dangerous to keep it,' Marc added sweetly.

'Er . . . quite—'

'When you drew a blank with the gold,' I said, 'you took it almost as a personal affront that Thévenon hadn't left it there. So you were glad of the chance to get your own back. If you hadn't sent the gun to the police, Monsieur Jander, Thévenon mightn't have died. But I don't think someone who'd been doing his best to appropriate gold bullion belonging to the Banque de France was in any position to point the finger at somebody else.'

'I was doing my duty.'

'Anonymously!' Marc spat out.

'Come on, Marc,' I said, getting up. 'We'll talk about that when we come back for the lecture on morals. Now let's get out of here. I've found out all I can.'

We went back to the car.

'I hope the English drop a bomb on him. He disgusts me,' said Marc. He's a remarkably sound chap for a journalist. 'Now where are we going?'

'The Banque de France,' I said. 'I trust you haven't forgotten how to pick a lock.'

It wasn't much of a cellar. A few logs, a small heap of coal and two old packing cases took up nearly all the space. A few dusty wine bottles glinted in the feeble light from a small barred window high up in one wall. The dusty panes overlooked a neglected garden.

Covet's torch soon revealed traces of the hiding place Thévenon had constructed and Jander had broken open, then clumsily resealed.

'You think it's in there?' said Marc sceptically.

'No,' I said. 'Only the revolver was in there. Nothing else *could* have been.'

'You're starting to sound like Sherlock Holmes. A good sign! A few more remarks like that and the gold will be ours. Perhaps you could make it come pouring out of those bottles.'

'Spoken like a true drunkard,' I said.

The corkscrew on my penknife went into action and we were soon swigging quite a respectable little wine.

'Didn't you notice something I said at our virtuous

friend's place just now?' I asked. 'I said it aloud just to see how silly it sounded.'

'Let me think . . . '

Marc frowned, and ran a finger up and down the bridge of his nose.

'There *was* something – yes. Oh, I know! About the incriminating evidence. You said it was safer in the wall than at the bottom of the river. I thought that was a bit much.'

'Why?'

'Er—'

'Have another swig. Maybe it'll bring it back.'

He seized the bottle almost before the words were out of my mouth. It did the trick.

'Because it's idiotic to hide incriminating evidence in the house you've been staying in. The police are bound to take the place apart if ever they discover it . . . A pond a couple of miles away from here would have been much safer.'

'Good thinking. Go on.'

'Oh no – that's enough for one day.'

'But may I ask a question?'

'Try.'

'Was Thévenon a fool?'

'True.'

'What's true?

'He wasn't a fool.'

'Nor am I,' I said. 'And now it's my turn to show how clever I am. Criminals know all about alibis. There are several kinds, and that hole there is one. Let me explain. In his hide-out Thévenon thinks of a way of concealing the gold so well that no one can find it. He needs to use cement to do the job, but there's a danger that if the investigators are thorough enough they'll come across the shopkeeper he bought it from, and in due course discover the hiding place itself. So he has to set a trap – let them find a *false* hiding place. When that yields up the only existing piece of incriminating evidence, they'll think that was all Thévenon had to hide, and promptly call off the search.'

'So the gold bars are still here somewhere?' said Marc.

'I've every reason to think so.'

'Why not in another part of the house?'

'Cement leaves marks. He wouldn't have risked sloshing it everywhere. The real hiding place can't be far from the false one.'

'We'll have to dig up the floor, check the ceiling—'

'No,' I said. 'That's too obvious. The CID would be bound to do that.'

'I see,' he chuckled. 'More thinking required, eh? You're very lavish with the little grey cells!'

'And you're very lavish with your batteries.' He kept waving his torch about as he spoke, and shining it in my eyes. 'Turn it off. We don't need to see.'

He did as he was told.

'You're right,' he said. 'I never miss my mouth in the dark.'

He had another go at the bottle, then adopted the position of Rodin's *Thinker* on one of the packing cases.

Our eyes gradually got used to the semi-darkness. The grey light seeping in through the open door and the little ground-level window seemed to grow brighter. Suddenly a ray of spring sunshine broke through the clouds, touching the garden with light and casting the shadow of the barred window on to the uneven floor. A small dark shape was moving between two of the bars. I looked up. A spider was spinning its web.

'How many ingots were there?' I said.

'Four. The easiest way to hide them would be—'

'Were they cylindrical?'

'Yes. But—'

My knife in my hand I leapt to the window and began scratching furiously at one of the bars. A layer of earth. A layer of paint. Then another ray of sunshine struck yellow-ish metal, bringing forth gleams of gold.

18 The murder weapon

Marc Covet dropped me off at the agency. He hadn't uttered a word all the way back. Seeing the gold bars had had the same effect on him as if he'd been hit over the head with them.

'I'm going back to the office,' he gasped. 'For once the showers are working. If I don't have a good long soak I'll explode.'

When I got upstairs Hélène and Reboul looked as if they were waiting for me. She said Pierre Friant had concocted a report as arranged, so I skimmed through it: it seemed all right. Reboul said he'd finally winkled out a witness to the accident in the rue Monsigny, and he was willing to come in whenever we liked: I said that evening would do. Then I asked Hélène to send Laurent Gaillard in to see me as soon as he turned up. When I mentioned him the scowl she'd adopted to talk about Pierre Friant disappeared, and her face lit up. She obviously had a crush on him. I left her to it and shut myself up in my office.

A quarter of an hour later my reflections were interrupted by the telephone. It was Marc Covet.

'We've just heard officially from the police that Madame Bourguet was the woman in the taxi.'

'Do you think that's the result of my anonymous letter?'

'It looks like it. But I've got some news on that front.'

'What sort of news?'

'Sorry to spoil your victory celebrations, but you were so brilliant this morning a little disappointment won't bother you.'

'Cut the cackle,' I said, 'and get to the point. I've got other things to think about.'

'Thinking isn't always your strong point. You were wrong all along the line as far as Madame Bourguet was concerned. When they got your letter the police carried out the usual checks, and there's no connection at all between the gun used to kill Barton and the one Madame Bourguet had. They're both 7.65 mm, but the slugs don't match. What's more, Madame Bourguet didn't leave her house on the 17th. There are at least five reliable witnesses who'll testify to it. So what do you say to all that?'

'Only those who do nothing are never wrong.'

'You sound like my grandmother. Another thing she always—'

I hung up before he could finish the folklore, and started pacing up and down the room. My mind was in turmoil, one question crowding in after another. Finally I managed to get to grips with one of the easier problems: what to think about the gold. I reached a decision, then lit a pipe by way of reward.

But as the flame of my lighter began to lick at the tobacco, a series of similar images sprang into my mind. I staggered under a sudden revelation. Marc might have a low opinion of thinking, but sometimes it delivered the goods.

I rushed out of the office.

In the rue Lecourbe I went into the building where I'd spent the air raid the previous Tuesday, showing the concierge my red, white and blue card. I'd used it in Mac's hotel to pass myself off as a policeman. Now I said I was an air-raid warden, and he was short-sighted enough to believe it.

I asked him to come down to the cellar with me – I had something to check up on. He agreed, and after looking around for a while in an officious manner I asked him if he'd mind taking part in an experiment.

I made him stand where I'd been standing during the air raid, then I turned the light out and went a little way down the corridor behind him. I took out my lighter, struck it, and after a second extinguished the flame. Then I asked him if he'd seen anything.

'Yes. You lit your lighter.'

'Did you see the glow?'

'Yes,' he said unenthusiastically, obviously used to the eccentricities of officialdom.

I went further down the corridor and tried again.

'You've done it again,' he said.

'Yes. But did you see anything or just hear the flint being struck?'

'Just heard it.'

'Thank you,' I said without moving. 'You can put the light back on now.'

He did so, and I looked around. I was standing in front of cellar number seven, the last one along the central corridor, and the only one with a gap between the top of the door and the frame.

The concierge told me it belonged to a tenant named Denis who lived on the third floor, to the right of the landing. He was bound to be in now because he was unemployed. From the concierge's tone this was obviously a permanent state of affairs. And Monsieur Denis never went out, not even to look for work.

I went up to the third floor and rang the bell. After a long interval Monsieur Denis opened the door. His face spoke volumes: he clearly thought I'd come to cut off the gas and seize his belongings. Just the same, he didn't look the gullible type, so I decided not to waste time.

'Downstairs I pretended I was a warden,' I said. 'And I fancy telling you I'm interested in archaeology. But you don't have to believe me. Anyway there's a hundred francs in it for you.'

His face, which had hitherto shown only anxious stupefaction, lit up at this.

'You don't look like a copper,' he said.

'No, but I can ask questions just as well. Have you been down to your cellar recently?'

'I brought the last of the coal up about a month ago. There isn't any wine, with the ration at only a litre a week.'

'So you haven't been down there for about a month?'

'About that.'

'Would you mind taking me down?'

He hesitated, so I handed over the hundred francs.

'An expensive way to open a door,' I said. 'I could have smashed the padlock, but I can't stand loud noises.'

'Come on, then,' he said, looking a bit bemused.

The door to cellar number seven creaked open and I shone my torch on the ground just inside.

'My God!' croaked Denis. 'Did someone tip you off? Was it an anonymous letter? I swear—'

'Don't worry,' I said. 'The *Militärbefehlshaber* won't find out about it.'

I bent down and picked up the Browning.

Back at the agency, after fitting a bulb that was powerful enough to blow all the fuses in the building, I settled down in the privacy of a boxroom to examine my find.

It was a 7.65 automatic with three shells missing from the magazine. Two had been fired and the third was still in the breech. From the degree of oxidization in the barrel it was clear it had been used recently. About four days ago, I guessed.

I didn't waste time looking for fingerprints because the user had worn gloves. But I did try to find evidence that it had been fitted with a silencer. There was none.

I went thoughtfully through to my office, slipped the Browning into a drawer and locked it. I didn't feel like taking it home. But almost at once I took the gun out again and wiped off my own prints. Then I locked it up once more.

I called Mac's hotel, and was told by the manager that he'd returned from what he called his 'tour' and gone straight back to work at the Médrano.

It was Saturday. That meant there was a matinée. I had an hour to spare.

I left some instructions for Hélène and set off to see the miniature knight errant.

On the way I bought a newspaper. The case of the 'Tragic Mistress' took precedence over news of the war. Julien Bourguet had been abandoned by his influential pre-war friends and was now being questioned by the CID. As for the Barton case, Martinot had given a press conference in which he hadn't divulged a single bit of real information.

19 Hour of reckoning

I had no luck in my search for the dwarf, and got back to the agency at about five o'clock. Hélène and Laurent Gaillard were there. They looked as if they were posing for one of those photographers who specialize in sentimental scenes.

'Go next door, would you,' I said to Prince Charming, and as he did so I picked up the phone and called the café opposite.

'I'd like to speak to Monsieur Reboul,' I said. 'He's there? Good . . . Hallo, Reboul? Bring Monsieur Thiry over, please.'

Hélène was looking at me strangely. Her instinct and my expression told her danger was afoot, though she didn't know why. I patted her on the cheek.

'Better look for another boyfriend,' I said quietly. 'This one's in trouble . . . Why not put an ad in the paper?'

When I rejoined Laurent Gaillard he was already comfortably ensconced in an armchair next door. I followed suit and we began to discuss the case I'd put him in charge of. Then suddenly I got up and opened the door. Reboul was standing there beside a serious-looking citizen with an umbrella: Monsieur Thiry, the ear-witness.

'Well?' I said.

'That's him,' said Thiry importantly. 'Exactly the same voice. There's no doubt about it. What's more' – he squinted hard at Gaillard – 'I recognize him. He and Chabrot often used to eat together.'

'What do you say to that, Monsieur Gaillard?' I said.

Gaillard had started up and put on his glasses. But it was too late for disguise. As he stared through the plain glass at the intruder, the stereotyped smile on his lips bore no relation to the savage look in his eye.

'Well?' I repeated.

Suddenly he leapt forward, knocking me aside and making for Hélène's office and the front door. Monsieur Thiry bravely barred the way with his brolly, and received a blow in the stomach that folded him in half and sent him flying. But the diversion just gave Reboul time to get out of Gaillard's way, and more by luck than judgement he hit the button that controlled the heavy metal curtain guarding the door on to the landing. The iron curtain came down just in front of the killer, blocking his escape, and he crashed right into it, throwing out a hand to stop himself and letting out a roar of pain.

I leapt on top of him, only to find Hélène on top of *me*.

'You brute!' she yelled.

I involuntarily wheeled round and slapped her. She buried her face in her hands and slumped on to a chair in tears.

I dragged Gaillard into my own office by the scruff of the neck and pinned him into a chair with my knee on his chest. His face was twisted with pain. His hand must have been giving him gyp.

'Thought you were clever, didn't you?' I panted. 'You wanted to find out what we were hatching at the Fiat Lux Agency, so you decided to send us some bogus clients. Fake policemen, fake victims, fake husbands with unfaithful wives – to cope with all that you assumed we'd have to take on extra help, and given the references *you* presented you'd be bound to get the job! It would take us some time to check up with Auguste across the demarcation line in Lyons, wouldn't it? That meant you had at least two weeks' grace, and someone with your charm could find out a lot in that time, especially if you made up to Hélène. You could have had her betraying me without even knowing it. Oh yes, your little game was much cleverer than Chabrot's. His desire to cut a dash might have ruined everything. But you more than made him pay for it.'

'Why don't you just shut up and call the cops?' he gasped as well as he could for my knee.

'Leave the cops out of this, sonny,' I said. 'You don't imagine I've done all this just to hand you over to *them*? I don't give a damn about Chabrot's murder – for two pins I'd congratulate you. That's how easygoing I am. But I don't like being taken for a ride, so when someone tries it on I arrange a little encounter like the one we had a moment ago, just to show them what's what. Not for any other reason – I know already why you got involved in all this. You wanted the gold, didn't you? Well, you can forget about it. *I've* got it, and I'm going to stick to it!'

I could see from his face that this possibility had never occurred to him. He let out an oath.

'If you've got the loot, what do you want me for?' he wheezed.

'Barton,' I said. 'You're going to tell me how you killed him.'

Gaillard's eyes nearly popped out of his head.

'What?'

'You're going to tell me how and why you killed Henri Barton.'

'But—'

'Better still, you're going to write it all down. We'll do it together, like a couple of journalists collaborating on an article. But I haven't got any literary aspirations. You can sign it. And when you've done that you can hop it. How's that for magnanimity?'

Reboul coughed, probably not for the first time, but it was the first time I'd taken any notice. Now he almost ruptured his vocal cords, not to mention touching me on the arm. I turned to see Monsieur Thiry still standing there. I'd forgotten all about him. He might be a bit shocked by what he'd seen of my methods.

I cast around for a way of intimidating him enough to keep him quiet. Then, summoning up all the German at my command, I barked out a rigmarole about no entry, goodbye and thank you, snacks available and do not lean out of the window. In answer to which Reboul, to my surprise, produced an impressive 'Jawohl!' and all but clicked his heels. During this performance we both prayed Thiry wasn't an expert in modern languages, but the apprehensive look on his face reassured us.

His evidence might get us into hot water later on, but for the time being he'd say nothing.

I was just congratulating myself on my stratagem when Laurent Gaillard brought me back to earth. Taking advantage of my temporary distraction he wrenched himself free and threw me flat on the floor. As I got to my feet I heard the door of the boxroom slam to. Gaillard was making for the roof. I rushed to the door only to find it bolted. Together Reboul and I broke it down. Inside, the table had been dragged into the middle of the room. Above it the skylight was open.

I pulled myself up and out on to the roof, and spotted my quarry eighty yards away. He was beyond the chimney of the house next door, moving as fast as he could on the slippery surface, his injured hand held up in the air.

Night was falling, and a typical February drizzle had started. The lights had been on for some time in the offices on the other side of the boulevard, and the blackout curtains were drawn. No one could see our antics. Just as well.

I was cursing Gaillard under my breath and trying to reduce the distance between us when, just as he reached a point where several windows offered him safety, there was suddenly an indescribable din overhead and a German aeroplane, its engine sputtering, swooped down in the way that seems to amuse Luftwaffe pilots, seemingly right on top of us.

Episodes flashed through my mind from films I'd seen in my childhood, with rope-ladders let down from planes to save Pearl White from fiendish Orientals. But this wasn't the cinema.

Far from saving Gaillard and carrying him off, the plane meant the end of him. Surprised by the racket, he looked up and lost his footing on the wet surface. I saw his mouth gape open, but his terrified shriek was inaudible. He began to roll down the sloping roof . . .

The gutter checked his fall for a moment, but the hand that tried to clutch at it was the injured one . . . The next thing I heard as the plane drew away were shouts of horror as the body of Q.E.D.'s killer crashed on to the pavement below.

Back at the agency Reboul and Hélène were alone. Monsieur Thiry had been sent home.

'Do you think he'll keep his mouth shut?' I said.

'Yes,' said Reboul. 'All he wanted to do was get out of here. He'll keep his mouth shut.'

'You two had better do the same. Gaillard fell off the

roof. The body's bound to attract the bluebottles even in this weather.'

Hélène began to sob again. I shrugged and went over to my desk. My eye was caught by a drawer that was slightly ajar – the only one with a key in the lock. I felt myself going pale, and swore as I wrenched the drawer open. The gun from the cellar in the rue Lecourbe had gone.

I rushed out and confronted Hélène.

'Who's been here apart from Gaillard?' I shouted. 'Who opened that drawer?'

She stopped dabbing her eyes and turned towards me, her face streaked with mascara.

'Who was it?' I bellowed, beginning to shake her. 'Answer me!'

'Faroux!' she shouted back. 'I'd forgotten. He came while you were away. First he insisted on waiting, and then he left. If he took something I hope it was because he suspected you! I hope he'll—'

She was so angry she couldn't go on, and buried her face in the handkerchief once more. I suddenly felt as if I'd been hit on the head. My fury abated. I stopped shaking her. Instead I began to pat her gently on the shoulder.

A police car went rushing down the boulevard, siren blaring. Another siren followed – an ambulance this time. Laurent Gaillard's last ride.

'You think it was my fault, don't you?' I murmured.

She removed my hand from her shoulder. I shook my head.

'I'm sorry,' I whispered. 'I told you to be careful about falling in love.'

I didn't add that I should have followed my own advice.

20 Heart to heart

The phone rang for the third time in less than half an hour.

'How long's this game going to go on?' said Lydia impatiently. 'Take it off the hook if you don't want to answer.'

She was half intrigued and half furious, and it made her more charming than ever. She was huddled next to the stove, trying unsuccessfully to read. I hadn't been very chatty since rejoining her, and my change of attitude hadn't gone unnoticed.

'That's right,' I said. 'Then whoever it is will know I'm here. They probably started calling before I got back.'

She pointed at the telephone, which was all that was required to set it off again.

'Do you know who it is?'

'Nestor Burma knows everything.'

I produced a packet of Gauloises.

'Being unfaithful to your pipe?' she said.

'They're for you.'

'I don't smoke.'

'You've got a packet of *Fashions* in your bag.'

'Oh, that's just to be like everyone else. I only have one occasionally.'

'Perhaps this is one of the occasions. Have one now – you've got a decision to make.'

'I don't understand.'

'You will. Barton really was killed by his ex-wife.'

'My sister?'

'Don't make me laugh. I'm not in the mood.'

I pulled a chair over, sat down next to her and took her hand.

'I've spotted you smoking several times. The first time in the air-raid shelter, the second in Bois-le-Roi, and the third coming out of my office. On each of those occasions you'd made or were about to make an important decision: in the shelter, the decision to get rid of the Browning because the old woman's story about the copper searching everyone had thrown a scare into you; in Bois-le-Roi, the decision to get rid of me; and, at the Agency, the decision, among others, to spin me a plausible yarn. On the day of the air raid you must have smoked another cigarette, too. Or rather, taken two or three drags as usual and thrown the rest away. It was picked up on Barton's staircase by one of the men in the demolition squad. You must have lit it just after doing Barton in.'

Her eyelids drooped and seemed to darken. The lobes of her ears were dead white.

'What have you got to say to that?' I insisted.

She kept her eyes lowered.

'You're as good as a fortune teller,' she said sarcastically. 'She reads palms, you read fingerprints.'

'There weren't any on the revolver if that's what you're worried about. You were wearing gloves, remember?'

'If I gave you a lock of my hair,' she went on as though I hadn't spoken, 'perhaps you'd be able to tell I was ill when I was ten because Father Christmas didn't bring me a doll.'

'I don't believe in Father Christmas. But I do have a certain faith in science. As far as the hair's concerned, I took a sample the first night you spent here. You can't be too careful, and a cop's a cop. I had it analysed, and I know its magnificent auburn is genuine. Whereas Jeanne Barton was a brunette. Or was, in 1938.'

'So why do you insinuate we're the same person? Do you think I'd ever dream of dyeing hair like mine?'

'Certainly not. It'd be sacrilege! I'm just thinking aloud, that's all.'

'Why, then?'

'Because of the illness you mentioned just now. It wouldn't have been typhoid by any chance, would it?'

She shrugged and didn't answer. But she looked paler than before.

'Let's say it *was* typhoid, then. You weren't ten when you had it – you were twenty. And one of the classic symptoms of typhoid is loss of hair. You decided to hide the damage under a black wig – raven hair had been in fashion since Conchita Moralès' visit to Paris – and you were so tickled with the result you had some photographs taken and gave them to a friend of yours. But this friend knew such things could be dangerous, so he got rid of them. Perhaps he threw them away – anyhow, someone else managed to get hold of them.

'This person *did* keep them – kept them as if they were holy relics. He was a dwarf, rather unbalanced sexually, and fell passionately in love with you. You were like a goddess to him. So much so that five years later he was ready to confess to a murder he believed you'd committed. Of course you never suspected his passion and Mac Guffine never declared it. It was just "the desire of the moth for the star" – certain to be rebuffed.

'But that didn't change the way he felt. Before getting

hold of the professional photographs you had taken he'd already taken at least one of you himself. It shows Jeanne Barton in intimate conversation with a man whose face is only partly visible. Barton? Thévenon, more likely. The dwarf used to follow him around like a puppy. So what does all this suggest? That you were pretty generous with your charms – not that I blame you for that, of course!

'So – you were Thévenon's mistress, and your husband didn't find out about it until after the hold-up at Le Havre. He was wild with rage, turned Thévenon over to the police despite the danger to himself. We thought he'd done it because he knew where the gold was and wanted it all to himself. No one dreamed it was a crime of passion – any more than they did when Barton was murdered last Tuesday.'

'All very amusing,' said Lydia.

'It's no laughing matter,' I said coldly. 'Don't overestimate your position. Nestor Burma's not such a brute as to denounce his mistress – that's what you're thinking, isn't it? Well, forget it.'

She slipped from her chair, wrapped fragrant arms around my legs and rested her head on my knees. She didn't say a word. Just looked up at me with enormous terrified eyes.

The telephone rang yet again.

'I'm not the only one involved,' I sighed, stroking her hair. 'The bloke who's trying to get through is a copper. A real one, with a moustache, paid by the state. He wants to ask me what the pistol that killed Barton was doing in a drawer at the Fiat Lux Agency. So it's not just up to me . . . A pity, because I think I love you.'

'I love you, too,' she whispered.

'You don't have to pretend. You've tricked me that way before.'

'I do love you, my darling. I—'

'Sure,' I said. 'Love at first sight, wasn't it? I'm irresist-ible—'

'No. You were right about the other night. I just wanted to—'

'You just wanted to nobble me . . . And like a fool I mentioned a sister, and that gave you an idea. I seemed to know a lot, but not everything, and you thought it wouldn't take me long to find out the rest. So why not lead me off on a false trail? Jeanne was a brunette and you're a genuine redhead – it was unthinkable that you would have sacrificed your magnificent head of hair. So I was bound to accept the existence of a sister. That would delay things, and by the time I found out the truth we'd be lovers!'

'From the way you looked at me it was obvious how you felt. I decided to take advantage of it.'

'Little whore!'

She gave a tired shrug.

'Insult me if you like. It may have been true until two nights ago. But not any more. Now I really do love you. I don't expect you to believe me.'

'Just as well. You've been leading me by the nose long enough. Between you and me I've been a bit slow on the uptake. Imagine me swallowing that sister business! Still, there were things you didn't know about that made it more plausible: Mac's confession, and the fact that there was another murder where a silencer was used.

'However, I hadn't lost my wits completely. When I saw Madame Bourget, everything seemed to point to her guilt, but I couldn't accept the idea of a woman using a silencer. Then I read in *Paris-Midi* that the prime suspect was a woman. So where did Mac's confession fit in? He must have made it up. Significantly, he only claimed to have murdered Barton when he was shown the banknotes smelling of the perfume he himself used. Why does he use the stuff, I asked myself – he may be emotionally twisted but he's basically normal. Could he have started wearing it just because it was the favourite scent of the girl he secretly idolized? If so, when he smelt the banknotes he must have thought he knew who the killer was, and decided to sacrifice himself for her. So who could she be?

'I turned the problem over and over in my head. Given my belief about women not using silencers, I concluded that if the killer was either Jeanne, Lydia, or Madame Bourguet the murder must have been committed – as the nitwits in the CID thought – during the air raid. That meant you lied when you said Barton was already dead when you found him. Then Marc Covet told me Madame Bourguet had shot herself and the gun she used was fitted with a silencer. So there was no doubt about it: she was the killer, the woman the police said they suspected, and what you'd told me about Barton was true.

'But I was wrong again! The investigators proved she didn't kill Barton, and they apparently never suspected she did. When I found this out you were already on my mind, and, forgive me for saying so, not for sentimental reasons, but in connection with a rather strange individual. Talking of which, did you have any particular reason for renting that villa out at Bois-le-Roi, or did you take it just by chance?'

She looked at me in amazement and couldn't answer.

I repeated my question.

'No particular reason,' she got out finally. 'I was part of the exodus from Paris when the Germans invaded, and when I tried to move back everything was taken. Even as far out as Bois-le-Roi that was the only house available.'

'What an extraordinary coincidence!' I said.

'What do you mean?'

'I'll tell you later, if Faroux gives me time. He hasn't rung for a while. Maybe he's on the way here with his squad.'

She shivered.

'The collapse of the Bourguet theory was a bitter blow,' I went on. 'I had to rethink everything. Among the rest, I went over every movement I'd seen you make. And suddenly, in a blinding flash, I saw! I rushed to the rue Lecourbe, all my old suspicions reviving about the sister you said was living in the unoccupied zone. What if she didn't exist and you'd simply adopted your second name, Lydia, when you'd started using your maiden name again? As for your hair, one of the newspapers from 1938 mentioned that Madame Barton had been ill. I remembered you missing your footing on the stairs, and that reminded me of the popular belief that typhoid affects people's legs . . . And typhoid would explain the puzzle of the hair as well . . .

'When I got to the rue Lecourbe I found the Browning. Obviously the murder weapon. But there were none of the tell-tale marks a silencer would have left!

'Back to square one. There seemed no answer to the conundrum about the time of death. Until tonight. You see, sweetie, I know a couple of things that you don't know. Firstly, why Barton wanted to see you, and secondly, the *exact* time you pulled the trigger. Like all murderers you had only a vague idea. It was five to eleven.'

For a moment I let myself enjoy her surprise.

'When I took into account what you'd already told me and my own mistakes about Madame Bourguet, everything fell into place. Barton met you and made an appointment, but he didn't bother to ask if the time of the appointment suited you. Did you work at the same job in 1938 as you do now?'

'No.'

'I thought not. Barton didn't realize you were an employee with *Irma et Denise*. He thought you were a customer.'

'A customer?'

'Yes. He thought you were rich – *very* rich. So anyway, you go to the rue Lecourbe and knock on his door. Barton's drunk too much the night before and is still in bed. He gets up hastily, you walk in, and with barely a word thrown down on the table the ten thousand francs you intend to keep him quiet with. What I don't understand is that they smell of a perfume you don't use.'

'I did in 1938. Thévenon loved it. I had an old handbag with me when I went to Barton's, and in the bottom there was a tiny bottle I'd forgotten about. It had been there for years. There was a lot of pushing and shoving in the Métro and it got broken.'

'So you don't deny any more that it *was* you?'

'Have I ever?'

'Tell me the whole story, then.'

'I didn't mean to kill him,' she whispered. 'Just get him to leave me in peace. I made it clear I'd be ready to make more payments from time to time, but only on that condition.'

'You must have been pretty scared of him to offer to go on paying indefinitely.'

'I don't know. He always got me to do what he wanted.'

'That's why he never bothered to find out your address. He was sure you'd come when he whistled.'

'When I found him waiting for me outside *Irma et Denise* I thought he must know everything.'

'He wasn't waiting for you. He *was* looking for you. It was sheer chance he bumped into you.'

'I didn't know that. But even if I had I think I'd have gone.'

'And despite this power he had over you, you had an affair with Thévenon?'

'Henri had made me suffer too much. I'd loved him mindlessly, like a little girl, which is really all I was. But it didn't take him long to disillusion me. It was very painful. Thévenon was kind and considerate. Different from Henri. But I don't think I ever really loved him.'

'So?'

'What do you mean?'

'What about Barton?'

'Oh yes . . . When he saw the money he just laughed. He said: "Don't pretend you don't know what I want," and started coming towards me. I realized he wanted to get his revenge by . . . by making me . . . '

'No,' said I, so tersely that she started.

She gazed up at me, her face furrowed with pain. She looked ten years older, her eyes were lustreless, her hands clutched at mine in desperation.

'I'm not lying,' she sobbed. 'I can't lie any more. I swear.'

'I wasn't accusing you of lying. I meant it wasn't you he was interested in. It was the gold. Or its equivalent in bank notes. Ten thousand francs! – no wonder he laughed! He'd always believed, as you were Thévenon's mistress, that you were the woman in the taxi. And everyone thought she knew the secret of where the gold was hidden. It never occurred to him that Thévenon had such a soft spot for the ladies he'd had more than one lover.'

There was a silence before she continued.

'I stepped back, tripped, and fell on my knees.'

'You've still got the mark. I'd put it down to your tangle with the Sloper and his mate.'

'As I fell I knocked against something hard in the jacket hanging on the back of the chair. I don't know what went through my mind, if anything. But I guessed what the something was – it can't have taken more than a second. I pulled the gun out of the pocket—'

'And the lining came with it.'

'—and fired. Twice.'

'At five to eleven, just as a German plane came roaring over the roof. That's such a common occurrence, none of the witnesses even remembered it.'

'He didn't even cry out. He just fell. I lost my head and kept hold of the gun. Perhaps I'd got it confused in my mind with the money – I forgot all about taking that back. All I could think of was that I was free. It had cost me dear and I intended to stay that way. That meant putting up a fight for it, and that's what I've been doing all this week. But now—'

'Now Faroux's got the gun,' I said, pacing up and down, 'and Martinot's giving interviews mentioning everything except the female suspect – which means to anyone who knows him that he's about to pin her down . . . There was no reason for Faroux to come to the agency – we'd nothing to say to one another. But why did he go through my drawers if it was just a social call? He obviously didn't expect to find what he did find – at least I hope not – but he must have been suspicious. They're closing in. We'll be caught like rats in a trap. My God!' I said, driving a fist into my palm and clenching my teeth, 'I was afraid something like this would happen, but I thought they'd give me more time. Everything I touch is starting to go wrong again. Even the chap I had lined up to carry the can for Barton's murder has slipped through my stupid fingers. But that wouldn't have worked anyway. Faroux already had the gun.'

Lydia looked at me with a mixture of hope and disbelief. 'You mean you wanted to—'

She burst into tears.

'Yes, I wanted to save you. I still do. I know I scared you a bit just now, but Nestor Burma couldn't let himself be made a fool of without evening the score just a little.'

I put my arm round her shoulders.

'I don't know whether you love me, Lydia. And it doesn't really matter. I love you, and that's why I'm doing this. Faroux's a chum of mine. He confiscated the murder weapon in the absence of any witnesses, which is quite irregular. Perhaps he doesn't intend to produce it straight away. I think he'll ask me for an explanation first. That's probably what he's been trying to phone about. He's not a bad sort. But he's a copper just the same – he won't be able to keep it secret long. There's no time to lose, my darling. They could come in a week or in two hours' time. Here – take this.'

I handed her a train ticket that Marc Covet had got hold of for me, then scribbled a few words on an envelope and gave her that as well.

'Take this train. When you get to Bordeaux, go to that address. It's another chum, but not the same kind as Faroux. He'll take you to the Spanish border and help you cross. Wait for me in San Sebastian. I'll join you there soon and we'll tour the country. How's that for a honeymoon surprise?'

She looked so flabbergasted I couldn't help laughing despite the seriousness of the situation.

'If you're wondering what we're going to live on, it's true I'm broke, but by the time I get to you I'll have a fortune. You remember the men who attacked you in Bois-le-Roi?'

'I'd almost forgotten them,' she said.

'They were part of a gang of crooks and blackmailers called Q.E.D. They must have found out Barton was back and thought he'd turned over Thévenon so as to pick up the gold himself. I imagine Barton snuffed it before they heard his version. I assume they'd known about you for a long time, too, and had your address. But it was only when they saw you talking to Barton on Tuesday – they must have been following his movements closely – that they started to think you knew about the gold, and that you were the woman in the taxi. They made the same mistake about you as he did. It's incredible how everyone got hold of the wrong end of the stick in this business. So once Barton was out of the running they turned their attention to you in case you had any inside information, and when I turned up at your house, that convinced them that you did. To think the Sloper and the boxer set up their torture chamber in your sitting-room! What a joke!'

I went on to tell Lydia what I knew about Q.E.D.'s recent activity. When I explained that her house was where Thévenon had lived, and that the bars in the cellar window were made of gold, she produced the biggest yelp of surprise I'd ever heard.

'And those bars are magic wands that will turn a hard-up detective and a young fashion designer into a pair of prosperous tourists!' I exulted.

'You're not going to keep them, are you?' she said indignantly.

'The vaults of the Banque de France are empty,' I said. 'That gold would feel lonely down there. This way it'll see the world.'

'But you can't—! It's—' she began. But I closed her mouth with a kiss. I wasn't going to take lessons in virtue from a murderess.

21 The wrong end of the stick

A few hours later I took Lydia to the station. We had no unpleasant encounters on the way, but I was relieved to see the back of the last carriage disappear out of sight. The Austerlitz station was as grim and noisy as ever, though dawn was breaking on a bright Sunday. I went outside, unable to shake off a vague sense of loneliness. Then I pulled myself together. Dynamite was what was needed now.

I made a call from a public phone and arranged to meet an acquaintance of mine, Coco Leatherjacket. To judge by the way he dressed you'd think he was in need of charity, and what's more if you'd offered him money he'd have taken it. But that didn't stop him being one of the most capable smugglers of precious metals in the business, with a handsome bank account in Switzerland. When I'd hung up I did the same as everyone else and went to spend the day in the country. I thought Bois-le-Roi would be nice.

I didn't get back until Monday morning, carrying four large sausages that would have made any inspector who asked me to open my briefcase go through the ceiling. Luckily I got back to Paris without incident, and went into a quiet café. The gloomy-looking manageress was grumbling to one of her customers.

'As if we didn't have enough to put up with already, with the war!'

The man answered without raising his eyes from his newspaper, but what he said made me prick up my ears. One glance at the paper was enough! My hair stood on end, I paid for my coffee, and charged outside. Abandoning the contraband to its fate I hailed a cycle-taxi and went straight to the agency.

Strangely enough after what had happened on the Saturday, Hélène was there. But I was too stricken to show my surprise, and anyway she seemed to have forgiven me.

'Heavens, boss! Whatever's the matter? Are you ill?'

'Call Marc – quick!' I gasped.

I threw the gold bars into a drawer and waited, my pipe clenched between my teeth.

'It's him,' she said, and handed me the receiver.

'Hallo, Marc?'

'Ah! Burma!' he said. 'I was beginning to get worried. I thought you were on that train.'

'Well, I wasn't. But is it true?'

'Yes. It was derailed near Angoulême. Thank God you weren't on it!'

'Were there many casualties?'

'A hundred and fifty, so far. But there are a lot of bodies trapped in the wreckage.'

'Can you give me the list of the victims they've identified?'

'Yes – I've got it here. It's quite short. But why—'

'Just read it out!'

'Gaston Aurenche,' he began. '13 rue—'

'Just the names. Is it in alphabetical order?'

'Yes.'

'The letter V, then.'

'There are four: Lucien Valet . . . Jean Vandame . . .

Paul Vauger – all they found of *him* was an arm, but it happened to be the one with his service disc on . . . It was more or less the same thing with the fourth victim, a woman. Only one arm, the shoulder and a bit of the head were intact. But she was still holding her handbag, and although it was partly burned it still had her identity card in it. Her name was Lydia Verbois.'

'Lydia Verbois!' I shrieked.

Then I hung up and sat looking blankly in front of me. All I could do was swear or cry, or both at the same time. But I didn't have the strength to do either, and it wouldn't have made any difference if I had. One arm, the shoulder and a bit of the head! I hadn't wanted her to go to prison, but that seemed like paradise in comparison.

Hélène came over and took my hand as if I was a child. 'Boss,' she said.

'You're a good girl,' I mumbled. It was all I could say.

I went into my office and closed the door.

One arm, the shoulder and . . .

The words went round and round in my head. I began to count to get rid of them, and when I reached a thousand I started over again. But it didn't work, and by the time Hélène told me Faroux had arrived I was in such a state the news came as quite a relief.

The inspector came bouncing in. His hideous brown hat looked even more incongruous than usual.

'So I've caught up with the invisible man at last!' he laughed. 'I waited here for you on Saturday afternoon in vain. You know why? Because I'd been playing Sherlock Holmes and wanted to let you know I was as crafty as you. Next time you send me an anonymous letter you'll have to be more careful.'

He whipped out the letter I'd typed at the *Crépu* and

then explained laboriously how he'd deduced I was the author.

'As soon as I had a minute free I came round to tell you. And also to ask how you came to know so much about this Madame Bourguet. But you weren't here . . . Anyhow' – he took out his tobacco pouch and waved it – 'it scarcely matters now' – he rolled himself a cigarette – 'now that we know who killed Barton.'

'Yes,' I whispered.

'Justice is satisfied. The case is closed.'

I nodded.

'I suppose you've seen the papers?'

'Yes.'

'Who'd have believed it, eh?' he growled. 'The time it took us . . . !'

I made a vague gesture.

'Quite a fellow!' Faroux gave a little chuckle.

'Fellow?' I said. 'What do you mean?'

'Good Lord!' he exploded. 'You must have been on the bottle yesterday. I should have guessed as much from the way you look. Drink doesn't seem to improve your wits, Burma. I'm talking about Barton's killer, of course!'

'I don't—'

'And you say you've read the papers! Yes . . . He fell off a roof not far from here on Saturday evening. And do you know who he was? Our old friend Fernand Gonin, the missing member of the train robbers' gang. He was going under the name of Laurent Gaillard, and the Browning 7.65 he used to kill Barton was in his pocket. The details aren't all quite clear yet, and perhaps they never will be. But he's undoubtedly the murderer. The theory that it was a woman didn't hold water, despite all the argument you built up about Madame Bourguet. We soon abandoned that idea.'

I felt as if the floor was opening up under my feet, just as the roof had seemed to give way under Gaillard's. By taking the revolver he had led me into a monstrous error of judgement. Lydia had never been suspected by the police, and now, thanks to me, she'd been blown to pieces.

I pushed myself slowly up from my desk. The muscles in my face were so tense they hurt. My pipe snapped between my teeth, and the bowl fell on to the desk and rolled across the blotter. I spat out the remainder of the stem, returning Faroux's stupefaction with a venomous glare. If only the accursed fellow hadn't come here on Saturday to show off his powers of deduction . . .

'Get out!' I said hoarsely.

'But my dear Burma—'

'Get out! And take this with you – you've earned it!'

I opened the drawer, grabbed the gold, and hurled it down in front of him.

One bar – the one I'd identified first – rolled slowly across the desk. There was a flash of gold as a sunbeam struck the metal, and then it fell on the floor at the Inspector's feet.

'The gold!' he said.

'Get that trash out of here!' I shouted. 'I'll explain later. Just leave me alone!'

Faroux had gone as pale as I was. He was half shocked, half scared. He picked up the bars and beat a hasty retreat.

I sat down and buried my head in my hands.

Through the open window came the joyous trill of a bird greeting the spring. Followed, like an echo, by a girl's innocent laughter.

I hauled myself up again and went and shut the window.

Other books by Léo Malet

Sunrise behind the Louvre £3.99

'The air was icy cold. A yellowish fog hung over Paris. But it would soon be gone. The sun was rising behind the Louvre . . .'

Stealing priceless works of art from the Louvre. Profitable work – if you can get it. But when there's a hitch between supplier and client, Nestor Burma is soon in the picture, with his fair share of dangerous, if beautiful, bedfellows . . .

It starts with one well-dressed corpse, wearing a fake Raphael for warmth. A man Burma is to meet again a few hours later – hastily leaving his hotel. It's not surprising he smells a rat from one end of the Palais Royal to the other.

The elegant 1st arrondissement of Paris is becoming littered with corpses – and it's all in the name of art . . .

The Rats of Montsouris £3.99

'Then, slowly, without quite knowing why, I retraced my steps. Was it because of the redhead or because of the man with the tattoo? I think on the whole, it was because of the redhead...'

A rendezvous with a fellow ex-POW leads Nestor Burma, dynamic chief of the Fiat Lux Detective Agency, to a dimly lit bar in the rue du Moulin-de-la-Vierge. A venue quite empty of both windmills and virgins...

What he finds there is his tattooed mate, now part of a gang of burglars called the Rats of Montsouris. But this particular Rat is on to something so big he can only trust Burma. And when someone betrays him, the question remains – what *are* the back streets of the 14th arrondissement hiding?

Burma, assisted by the beautiful Hélène, is in for a string of seedy surprises...

Mission to Marseilles £3.99

'This was the first time he'd had a social call from a ghost. But any excuse would do for a bender . . .'

Marseilles 1942. A case of incriminating love letters solved, Nestor Burma heads back to Paris and his next assignment. But as the train glides into the Gare de Lyon, a corpse in the compartment arouses curiosity . . . And Burma receives an offer from the Gestapo he'd be foolish to refuse . . .

Playing dead's not easy for a PI nicknamed Dynamite. It's enough to drive a man to drink! But the ravings of a madman, and fierce professional pride will soon lead Burma back to unoccupied France and the mysterious Formula 5 . . .

It's the stickiest undercover job Burma has ever attempted . .

120 rue de la Gare £3.99

'We'd arrived in Lyon, Lyon-Perrache station to be precise. It was two o'clock by my watch and I had a nasty taste in my mouth . . .'

Nestor Burma has seen a lot of strange men die in his time. So when a soldier without a name utters the dying words "120 rue de la Gare", the chief of the famous Fiat Lux Detective Agency is only mildly intrigued.

It's when a colleague meets death gasping the same phrase that Burma's interest – and fury – are fully aroused. Time to take out his pipe, discover the secret of the morbid address and nail the murderer in one fell swoop.

One problem. Where is 120 rue de la Gare?

All Pan books are available at your local bookshop or newsagent, or can be ordered direct from the publisher. Indicate the number of copies required and fill in the form below.

Send to: **CS Department, Pan Books Ltd., P.O. Box 40, Basingstoke, Hants. RG21 2YT.**

or phone: 0256 469551 (Ansaphone), quoting title, author and Credit Card number.

Please enclose a remittance* to the value of the cover price plus: 60p for the first book plus 30p per copy for each additional book ordered to a maximum charge of £2.40 to cover postage and packing.

*Payment may be made in sterling by UK personal cheque, postal order, sterling draft or international money order, made payable to Pan Books Ltd.

Alternatively by Barclaycard/Access:

Card No.

Signature:

Applicable only in the UK and Republic of Ireland.

While every effort is made to keep prices low, it is sometimes necessary to increase prices at short notice. Pan Books reserve the right to show on covers and charge new retail prices which may differ from those advertised in the text or elsewhere.

NAME AND ADDRESS IN BLOCK LETTERS PLEASE:

....

Name ——————————————————————————————

Address ————————————————————————————

——————————————————————————————

——————————————————————————————

——————————————————————————————

3/87